# CURSED MAGIC

## REJECTED FATE TRILOGY
## BOOK 2

### JEN L. GREY

# CHAPTER ONE

The iridescent shadow that it seemed only I could see moved closer to the door of the small cabin where my sister had been held captive.

As I kept my eye on the enemy, a peculiar warmth jolted through my blood, but the cold fear this strange occurrence would usually trigger couldn't take hold of me.

With each step away the shadow took, the intense pressure on my body lessened marginally.

Ryker groaned where he lay crumpled after taking the knife strike that had been intended for my sister. His three pack members stood in front of their alpha, snarling and growling, unable to see the threat that had moved to the opposite edge of the room.

Warm blood flowed down one of my hands and dripped from my fingertips to the cheap floor, another reminder that no one but me could see our adversaries. When I'd gripped the back of the shadow's neck while it had been trying to kill Kendric, the shadow had managed to slash my wrist.

Thanks to the strange magic currently buzzing through my body, I couldn't feel the pain.

All I knew was that Ryker had gotten stabbed badly enough to bring him down, and my sister had to be weak from captivity. This had to end now.

"You fucking coward!" I exclaimed as I balled my hands and allowed unbridled rage to consume me. Ever since my pack had been slaughtered, I'd relished the hard shell my adrenaline and fury gave me. "You hide behind shadows and refuse to reveal your face to us."

The shadow flinched like I'd hit a nerve.

Good. I wanted to see which Blackwood pack member this person was.

I stepped in its direction, but Briar climbed to her knees and wrapped her arms around my legs the way she used to do to our parents when she was a child.

"Em, no," she begged as the shadow inched toward us— in no hurry. Even though the shadow was still here, none of us could rely on our senses to track it because its scent was too faint, and being closer to it didn't help.

I glanced down at Briar, seeing the greasy, light-copper hair on top of her head. "Let me go," I muttered, needing to attack the shadow before it got too close. "It's coming toward us again."

Another groan came from Ryker as he straightened from the floor, the knife protruding from his side as blood spilled down his black shirt. His normally olive complexion was a shade paler, and his expression looked strained from what I was sure was pain. "Protect Ember with your life."

My heart squeezed uncomfortably, but my feelings for him were something I could address only if we made it out of here alive. Unfortunately, the track record for people surviving these attacks was not in our favor. The only survivors I knew of so far were Briar and me.

The dirty-blond wolf on Ryker's right—Gage—turned

his huge head toward me and nodded. I didn't have to pack-link with him to understand he would obey his alpha's command. However, Kendric's black wolf and Xander's dark-brown wolf remained in place, flanking Ryker.

All four of these guys were idiots, and the shadow was once again right on us. "None of you can see it, only I can, so Briar, let me go, and the four of you get out of the way, or you're going to wind up even worse off."

The shadow's shoulders shook as if it were laughing, making me want to claw its eyes out. Whoever it was didn't mind being called a coward and enjoyed having power over us. After my fated mate Reid Blackwood had rejected me in front of both our packs, that motivation seemed in line with what was going on here. "He's taunting me—everyone, stay where you are."

Now the shadow was only five feet away.

I yanked at Briar's arms, and she dropped her hands. I pushed her so she fell on her back, closer to Ryker, Kendric, and Xander.

My chest constricted, but keeping her alive and out of reach of the shadow was my priority.

"Dammit, Ember," Ryker snarled, but Kendric and Xander closed in around him, preventing him from moving forward.

I had no time to deal with Ryker. The shadow moved toward me suddenly, and I pivoted to the right, away from Gage, not wanting him to get hurt.

Clearly, the shadow hadn't expected that, and it ran into air in the place I'd been standing. It spun toward me, and I kicked it with my right leg, trying to push it away from everybody.

It stumbled a few steps and tripped over Briar's legs.

Gage kept blinking hard as if that would make the figure magically appear.

Briar screamed and swung her legs, sweeping the shadow's feet from underneath it. It thudded to the ground.

Gage pounced just as the shadow got up quickly, causing him to land on the cheap laminate floor with a loud *thud.*

I dropped my shoulder and charged the shadow. I had to get it away from everyone.

"Ember, no!" Ryker exclaimed as he shuffled toward me.

I ran into a muscled body that felt male. Its scent didn't get stronger—it smelled faintly of shifter, and there was nothing else mixed in with the musk, which made it being one of our own the only option.

So why cloak its smell at all?

As I rammed the shadow into the wall, sharp claws dug into my back.

"I've got a hold of him, and he's right against the wall," I rasped, hoping that Gage could assist me.

The nails dug in deeper, and my back throbbed, but I didn't let go.

Snarls came from behind me, and Ryker yelled, "Move *now.*" Alpha will radiated from him in waves, and a few taps of Gage's paws scratched the floor.

From the corner of my eye, I saw Gage hunker down to attack and Ryker run past Kendric and Xander.

That was enough distraction for the shadow to best me. As Gage leaped toward us, it kicked me in the stomach then elbowed me in the back. I dropped onto all fours just as Gage reached it.

"Watch—" I started to yell when the shadow grabbed

Gage by the throat and lifted him so that his paws dangled in midair.

Gage's blue eyes bulged, and he swiped his front paws at the shadow.

Ryker shuffled forward, the knife still protruding from his side, and Xander rushed toward Gage.

The shadow moved, dragging Gage's body as if they were dancing despite the gasping wolf trying to catch his breath. It used Gage as a shield while Xander tried to figure out where the shadow was actually located.

Ryker reached me, Kendric glued to his side. Ryker kneeled and touched my injured back. His palm eased some of my agony. "We've got to get you and Briar out of here."

I shook my head, trying to ignore my throbbing back as I climbed to my feet. "You and Briar need to leave." I understood that he wanted to protect me, but I had the urge to knock him unconscious and drag his ass out of here.

Ryker reached for my arm, but his injury and blood loss impacted his speed, so I was able to dodge and kick at the shadow's legs once again. This time, it twisted so that I kicked Gage in the side, and his body swung, putting more pressure on his neck.

The shadow was anticipating my moves. I had to change my strategy.

I pretended to kick again, and the shadow moved so Gage was between us once more. Tapping into my speed, I rushed around Gage and punched the shadow in the side of its head.

My fist connected with bone, and the shadow's head snapped to the side, allowing me to drop my arm and break its grip on Gage.

Gage crashed to the floor, chest heaving and tongue lolling out, trying to catch his breath.

The shadow turned, and I assumed it was looking at me. It lunged within a second and whipped its hand toward my neck. I jumped back, my foot catching Ryker's leg, causing me to stumble.

"Fucking Fate, Ember," Ryker snarled, but I managed to catch my balance and surge toward the door of the cabin.

If I could lead it outside, then maybe the others would be safe. They might be able to get away like Briar and I had managed last time. Kendric, Gage, and Xander would be more willing to leave me behind to protect their alpha, especially since Ryker's power was draining with the loss of blood, and I could alpha-will Briar to leave me.

I didn't have a chance to feel sick about considering that because the shadow charged right at me, hand lifted, making its intentions known—it wanted to slash my throat.

It had an affinity for using its claws like I did for kicking during a fight, something we seemed to pick up about each other. Whoever I was fighting was smart—they must be from a strong pack.

I gritted my teeth, waiting till the last millisecond to make my move. Briar let out a bloodcurdling scream at the exact moment that I dropped to my knees. The shadow hadn't anticipated that, probably because it wasn't used to being even semi-visible to anyone, and its body slammed into mine.

I took the impact, doing a backward roll and landing on my feet. When they touched the floor, I raised my hands and stood straight up, throwing the shadow's body off me. It flew over my head and into the wall behind me, next to the door.

A loud whistle pierced my ears, and I clapped my hands over them. It didn't do much to drown out the noise.

The shadow stood and quickly moved to the door.

No. I couldn't let it escape. This person had to die. It had hurt my pack, my friends, and Ryker. I was *done* not fighting back.

Gritting my teeth, I snagged what felt like its shirt. I took a deep breath, realizing that this person had to have mastered the art of shifting better than anyone in my pack ever had, managing using only its claws while still dressed and in human form.

Moans of pain came from the others, but the whistle stopped.

When I yanked the shadow back, it turned sideways and plowed its shoulder into my body, ramming me against the wall. I kicked at it just as sharp claws dug into my stomach. I whimpered, unable to hold in the noise as it continued to push its claws deeper.

I had to get out of this hold, or I'd die.

I wrapped an arm under its head, putting it in a choke hold, then dug in my fingers and touched the hard part of an Adam's apple.

The shadow was definitely male.

Kendric and Xander surged toward us, but the shadow bent down and threw me over its head.

I landed hard on my back, pain exploding through me. My stomach convulsed in a way I'd never experienced before, but I didn't have time to give up.

Both Kendric and Xander reached me at the same time Ryker and Gage stumbled toward me. Briar was huddled in the corner with her eyes closed, rocking back and forth.

I sat up just as the shadow opened the door. He was eager to get away rather than finish the job, and I wondered why.

Whatever the reason, it couldn't be anything good.

My stomach dropped, and I pressed a hand to it as I

climbed to my feet. I tensed, anticipating more shadows racing in, but my attacker merely slipped outside.

What the hell?

I groaned, my insides feeling like they were going to come out. By the time I was fully upright, both Ryker and Briar had reached me.

"Where's the attacker?" Ryker asked, searching the room for a person he couldn't see.

"He went outside." I shook my head, trying to clear it of pain and confusion. I couldn't fathom why he'd gone.

"He?" Briar panted. "Could you see his face?"

"When I choked him, I felt his Adam's apple. I couldn't see him fully—it was more like watching an iridescent sheen." I shuffled to the door and looked for other shadows.

There were none.

Strange.

A shiver ran down my spine. We had to get out of here —staying would be the equivalent of a death sentence. "Let's go. The coast is clear for now."

Ryker's forehead lined with worry, but he nodded.

Gage shook his entire body, his blond fur swaying as the group came together at the door.

I stepped out first, scanning the area one more time.

Still nothing.

"Let's go," I whispered, afraid to gesture too much with the way my stomach felt right now.

I led the group, continuing to scan for signs of shadows.

A few shifters lay dead on the ground with their throats ripped out, the scent of their blood thick in the air. Memories of my pack members flashed through my head as grief tried to take hold, but I pushed it away.

I couldn't break down now. I had to get Briar to safety.

Our group walked across the grassy open area to the

woods at a near crawl. We needed to move faster, but between Gage, Ryker, and me, this was the best we could do. I remembered how Dad used to tell me, *Slow and steady wins the race*.

Once we reached the tree line, hope swelled in my chest. Maybe we would get away after all.

But when we weren't even a hundred feet into the woods, footsteps padded behind us...more than one set.

They'd come back to finish us.

## CHAPTER TWO

My heart pounded, and a sour taste filled my throat. My gaze landed on Ryker, who was now being carried by Xander and Kendric, still in their wolf forms. Even from this angle, I could see that his eyes were closed like he'd passed out, and blood was pouring down his side into Kendric's fur. I wanted to remove the knife, though I understood why he hadn't. It would cause worse bleeding, and we needed to control the injury as best we could.

But he was fading.

My throat constricted, and I pushed the odd sentiment away and focused on Briar. She'd stayed right behind them, in front of Gage and me. Her gait was slower than normal, but at least she was upright and moving.

Gage limped beside me, still impacted from being choked nearly to death.

Faint footsteps sounded like they were following us.

When I stopped, it took Gage a second to notice. He let out a huff, and the others stopped and looked back at me.

He tilted his head, and somehow, I understood the question without being able to pack link with him.

"Keep moving. Get to the vehicles before they catch up to us again." They were wasting precious time right now. With two of them having to carry Ryker, we'd been moving a whole lot slower than we should have been. Every second we delayed made it less likely that we'd make it out of here.

Briar's brows furrowed. "Why did you stop?"

"Do you not hear that?" Footsteps were shuffling around the same location like they were trying to catch our scent to hunt us down. I didn't understand why none of them could hear it.

I swallowed and tipped my head back. Was I hallucinating again, like the time I'd thought we were being watched in the national park when Ryker, Xander, and Kendric had been searching for Simon, the vampire we'd found outside the nest that had just been slaughtered?

"Hear what?" Briar blinked a few times and gazed around.

"The footsteps," I gritted out, needing everyone to start moving again. "Everyone needs to get to the vehicles as quickly as they can." I waved my hand forward.

"We only stopped because you did. Let's go then." She took a step forward, but when I remained in place, she didn't continue.

I saw she was going to make this difficult, so I locked eyes with Gage and said, "I'm going to stay back and hold them off. Can you guard my sister and lead the way back to the cars? You two can move quicker than those two can with Ryker, and Briar has no idea where we parked."

There was no point in the five of them staying when they couldn't even see the attackers. I just needed to distract the shadows long enough for them to get to the car...which wasn't very likely, but I refused to hand all of us over for easy slaughter.

"Absolutely not." Briar shook her head. "I'm not going anywhere without you."

"Yes, you are." I'd resented Dad for making Briar and me run when our pack got annihilated. He'd used his alpha will on us, and I'd had so much anger and resentment over it. Now all of that dissipated because, in this moment, I understood exactly why he'd done what he did—he'd had to make sure the two of us had a chance at being safe and making sure our story was heard.

I didn't want Briar to hold that same resentment toward me. "Move. Now," I ordered, my wolf inching out, ready to lace my words with power if needed.

Briar's jaw twitched.

Normally, Briar was complacent and didn't challenge authority. I wasn't sure if her newfound stubbornness was due to me being her sister or because we'd lost our pack, but it didn't matter. I was her alpha, and this was one thing she'd be forced to obey.

My wolf surged forward, and Briar's eyes widened.

Guilt weighed on my chest, but I pushed it away. Keeping her safe and giving her a chance to live was more important than her potentially hating me for the rest of her life.

Power like I'd never felt before radiated through me, and my words echoed as I spoke. "Run to the car as quickly as you can. And leave."

The footsteps began moving in our direction and in a more consistent pattern. The pressure around my body began to build once again. I didn't understand why none of them seemed to hear anything.

Briar's face twisted in agony, but her wolf forced her to obey my command. *I'll never forgive you for this,* she linked, the sting of betrayal coursing through our bond.

Not able to handle sensing any more of her emotions or hearing the insults she might toss my way, I closed the link between us.

If I thought she couldn't have been hurt worse, boy, had I been wrong.

Her nostrils flared, and her eyes turned glassy with unshed tears before she ran.

Still, it was enough for Xander and Kendric to pick up their pace again. I'd had no doubt they'd obey. It wasn't like they could help fight with Ryker on their backs, and the best way to protect their alpha was to get him away from here.

I couldn't think about Briar's struggle to fight the command, so I refocused on Gage. "Please protect her."

He nodded and took off after Briar and the others, and suddenly, my lungs could work again.

Half the problem had been fixed, but the harder part of the equation was coming now.

I faced the direction of the attackers and flexed my fingers. The congealed blood on my right hand and finger-tips felt sticky and nasty. I preferred that to the warm trickle that continued down my back from the injuries the shadow had given me. Hopefully adrenaline would help numb the agony soon.

I rolled my shoulders, trying to loosen my muscles for the inevitable fight. All that did was send a sharp stabbing sensation coursing down my back as if I'd ripped the skin and muscles further. This was going to be painful, but I had to push all that shit aside to protect my sister and friends.

My wolf howled inside me, not liking the idea of sitting here like a wounded animal. I wanted to shift so I could fight more easily, but with my injuries tearing more just from moving, shifting wasn't possible. I bit the inside of my cheek as my pulse pounded in my ears, the sound almost louder than the footsteps coming toward me. The pressure against my body grew more uncomfortable than ever.

A large number of them must be heading my way.

A strange ripple floated through my limbs, similar to what I'd felt in the woods when I'd thought we were being watched. My gaze darted left where the sensation seemed to be coming from, but once again, nothing looked out of the ordinary.

Well...other than shifters looking like shadows to me and remaining completely invisible to everyone else. What sort of magic had the Blackwoods gotten involved with? I hadn't known a spell like that was even possible.

The footsteps were upon me. The shadows weren't bothering to be quiet as they swarmed into the clearing.

My heart stopped.

There were at least twenty I could count and only one of me.

Though they didn't appear to have weapons, I'd learned that their weapons would be invisible until they removed them from whatever was hiding them. Plus, they could use their claws.

Refusing to give up, I looked around and found a decent-sized branch that had fallen from a nearby oak tree. I grabbed it and held it up like a baseball bat.

I'd take as many of these fuckers down as I could before I went down myself.

Two shadows came at me at the same time, and I ran forward, ignoring the torture of the burning pain in my back, and swung the branch at the first one's head. It lurched away and knocked into the one beside it.

That was the only good news. The other eighteen charged at me as a group.

Adrenaline coursed through my body, easing some of

the pain. I focused on what was in front of me. I lifted the branch back up, body screaming, and swung at the closest shadow to me. This one ducked and ran right into my stomach. I fell on my back with its entire weight on top of me, trying to suck in a breath to scream. I couldn't, and I wasn't sure if it was due to the weight or the torment.

I tried to shove the shadow off, my back feeling as if it were tearing in two. Tears ran down my cheeks as I used every bit of strength I had to push the bastard away. Two more shadows were now beside me, and blades appeared from behind their iridescent forms.

This was it.

The moment my life ended.

Still, I wouldn't quit. I'd die trying to win, even with the odds stacked against me. I had to keep them from reaching the others.

I managed to throw the shadow on top of me into a tree, but the next two struck in unison.

I tensed, prepared for the inevitable pain, when all of a sudden, they both pulled their knife strike about two inches from my body. Tingles exploded around me, and the uncomfortable pressure that came with the shadows faded away.

*What?* I blinked several times, trying to comprehend why they weren't finishing the job. Were they trying to confuse me or playing some sort of cruel game?

More shadows crowded around the two that hadn't finished me off. The two reared back, and I rolled away, hoping to put some distance between them and me. Agony from the wounds in my back had me damn near tears.

The shadow on my right groaned as I pushed myself up and stood. I planted my feet shoulder-width apart, ready to fight, and the shadows moved toward me, but after two steps, the front ones stopped moving, and the ones behind them ran into them. Even as their bodies collided, the front pair didn't get any closer to me.

Like there was some sort of barrier between us.

What the *hell* was going on? The pressure had entirely vanished, and only the strange prickling remained. The sensation of new magic rearing its head confounded me.

I needed to understand what was happening, but I wasn't going to figure it out now. I would take advantage of whatever *this* was and try to catch up with Briar and the guys.

Spinning on my heel, I took off after them, glancing in the direction the sensation of being watched seemed to come from. Once again, nothing looked amiss.

I had to be losing my damn mind, and yet, like it had in the woods the other night, something urged me to go over there—like something *familiar* was there.

*No.* I didn't have time for this. Whatever was keeping the shadows back might not do so for much longer. I had to go.

Calling my wolf forward using the warm, animalistic magic I knew as well as my human soul, I paid attention to that power. Despite my back screaming in agony, each step got easier until I finally broke into a run.

I glanced back, expecting the shadows to be right on me, but they weren't.

Soon, the scents of Briar and the guys became stronger, and I could hear their faint panting. My shoulders loosened as I reopened my link back to Briar, not wanting them to think someone else was chasing them. *I've almost caught up to you.*

Cold tendrils of fear and the heat of anger came at the same time as she responded, *Are you okay?*

The icky feeling of guilt built in my chest—for what I'd done to her but also for realizing I shouldn't have shut down our connection. What if other shadows had been stalking them through the woods and she'd needed to contact me? Dad would've thought of that, which further proved that I wasn't ready to be an alpha...and yet, here I was. *I'm fine but don't slow down. We need to hurry.* Even as I linked it, I glanced back, expecting to see the shadows. They weren't there.

Something wasn't right about this.

Xander and Kendric, carrying a still-limp Ryker on their backs in tandem, came into view just as I heard whispers from the direction of the car.

Fuck.

We were walking into a trap.

*Don't go to the vehicles!* This had to be a trick to herd us to our deaths. Make us believe we were safe then kill us all.

After Reid had rejected me, I'd learned that humiliating people was something he enjoyed.

*What? Why?* Briar linked and then spoke aloud, "Ember said to not go to the vehicles after all."

If I could hear her speak, that meant the shadows could too. *Don't say another word. Turn around.*

*What are you talking about? You're behind us!* Her anger intensified, making my chest feel hot. She again spoke out loud. "She's insistent, but I—"

"Did you hear that?" a man's voice asked as if he'd suddenly decided it wasn't worth hiding in the shadows any longer.

My blood turned cold. When they'd stayed hidden, I'd been more confident that there *could* be some survivors. If we saw their faces, it probably meant our lives were over.

Kendric and Xander stopped and turned carefully

around, prepared to run back in my direction. Briar and Gage appeared behind them, my sister's face lined in pure panic.

*What do we do?* she asked, her eyes meeting mine.

That was the problem. I didn't know. This would be a good damn time for Ryker to come to once again.

As if Fate wanted to give me her middle finger, footsteps pounded in our direction, moving at a speed that shouldn't be possible for shifters.

A lump formed in my throat.

There was no way we were getting out of this.

I glanced around for some sort of weapon, but it was too late. The enemy was here. It was time to finally see who was behind the veil.

My allies and my sister ran quicker, but it was no use. The footsteps were gaining on them.

And the person chasing them who came into view first had me dropping to my knees.

# CHAPTER THREE

My lungs forgot how to work as every ounce of strength left me. That reaction should have terrified me, but seeing Kendric's vampire girlfriend, Raven, made me feel like we finally had allies we could trust.

Her long black hair floated behind her as she ran at vampire speed, her cognac eyes warm against her dark eyeliner. I could almost feel the concern flowing off her.

All that relief deserted me when Lucinda, Bella, and Martin—the vampire queen Ambrosia's top three guards—appeared behind Raven with even more vampires following them. Those three would take the first opportunity to kill the six of us.

"Stay back!" Briar snarled and tensed, preparing to fight.

I almost corrected her, but the way the three guards' eyes narrowed and their noses wrinkled with disgust had me second-guessing. The three of them could easily turn on Raven.

"We're here to help." Raven lifted a hand and stopped. "We know your sister and the Grimstone pack."

Briar's strangled laugh had me jumping to my feet once again. Between maniacal peals of mirth, she croaked, "My sister would—"

"It's true," I rasped, the words feeling like sandpaper against my raw throat. "We're staying with them."

Briar's head whipped in my direction, her color draining. She lifted both brows. "Are you serious right now?"

Hurt pierced my heart. My sister was looking at me like she didn't recognize the person I was, and honestly, I couldn't blame her. I didn't feel much like myself anymore. The night our pack was murdered, something inside me had changed fundamentally because all I wanted to feel was anger. "The Grimstone pack found me and took care of me, and they trust these vampires. I didn't know who was working with Reid and didn't know which packs I could trust, so yes, I've been staying with the vampires."

Xander exhaled, and his four wolf legs wobbled. I wasn't sure how much longer he and Kendric could keep carrying Ryker.

From this angle, I could see Ryker's pale face. His normally warm-brown scruff appeared black because of how much blood he'd lost, and the smell of copper hung heavy in the air. A panic-like pressure built in my chest. "We need to get to the vehicle and get Ryker mended before he loses more blood."

I hadn't realized how dire his situation was until this moment. He'd been moving well until we'd left the cabin... Had I known he needed immediate assistance, I would've handled the situation even more urgently.

Raven's attention zoned in on Ryker, and her eyes widened. "I thought the strong smell of blood was coming from you." She pointed at me.

Briar scoffed. "They could be watching us *right now,*

and we wouldn't know it. If we don't move, we could *all* end up like him." She bit her bottom lip and scanned the area.

She was right. Even though I was super relieved that Raven was here, that didn't mean we were safe. "We need to get back to the vehicles and go."

I didn't feel that weird heaviness, nor did I hear footsteps running toward us, but that could change at any moment. Although, in fairness, I wasn't sure if the damp, uncomfortable pressure I'd been feeling sporadically was caused by our attackers or if my mind was playing tricks on me.

"If it's just the Shae pack, we'll be fine." Raven straightened her shoulders. "They won't want to anger Queen Ambrosia by harming her people when we're here just to check on her friends."

"I wish it was the Shae pack, but it's not." We were wasting time standing here, and every second caused Xander, Kendric, and Gage to lose more of their strength and Ryker to creep closer to dying. "We can tell you everything back at the mansion."

"If these are the people who attacked our nest, we shouldn't leave." Lucinda removed her sword from her side, her blonde hair falling over her shoulder.

We didn't have time for this power play when the six of us were weak, hurting, and in need of healing. I inhaled deeply, taking a second to collect and calm myself. "If we could see them, then, yes, you'd have a point, despite your *allies* being severely injured and one important alpha near death." I had no issue reminding them of who we were supposed to be to them, per the vampire queen. "But you won't be able to see them—that's how they've been able to kill entire packs and a huge nest in a busy town without anyone seeing them coming. If you want to stay, be my guest, but the six of us need to go somewhere safe before our attackers can finish what they started."

I wasn't sure how Kendric and the others would respond to my stepping up since Raven was more integrated into their group than I was. I wasn't the leader, but Ryker was incapacitated, and I was the only alpha left standing... or near enough to standing.

When Gage took off with Briar toward the vehicle, some of my worry melted away. I should've known that the need to get Ryker medical attention would trump any other concerns. They'd lost almost their entire pack; they weren't going to risk losing him unless something detrimental to our species was happening.

Kendric and Xander didn't hesitate, still working together to carry Ryker, following after the two. Their gait was slower, revealing their fatigue but steady.

I picked up my own pace, and each time my body jarred, I could've sworn a knife stabbed me in the back. As I passed, the vampires scowled at me. All except one.

Raven pursed her red lips. "I'm heading back with the wolves. I agree with Lucinda that the rest of the vampires should remain and try to determine what happened here. Queen Ambrosia would want that. But if you get attacked and there is no way to win or protect yourself, retreat immediately."

Curling a lip, Martin stared at Raven with dead eyes that somehow darkened even more with dislike. "I understand that Queen Ambrosia put you in charge of the alliance with these mutts, but that doesn't include you making strategic decisions. Besides, twenty of our guards split off from us and are already in the pack neighborhood. We would never leave them behind."

When I'd met the three guards when we first arrived at

the vampires' mansion, I hadn't liked any of them. They'd made it clear that they weren't happy about the alliance between Ryker and their queen. However, I hadn't expected such animosity to be tossed Raven's way when she was clearly favored and trusted by their queen.

Still, I would keep my nose out of their argument because getting involved would only cause more problems for the six of us—er—no...

Not the six of us.

Briar and me.

I couldn't start thinking beyond Briar and myself. The Grimstones weren't my pack or my responsibility. I had to get my sister away from all this chaos and keep her safe. I couldn't lose her.

Yet, thinking about leaving Ryker and his pack made an uncomfortable knot settle in my stomach.

I couldn't contend with that now. Not while everyone was tired, injured, and still at risk of being attacked at any second. I wasn't even sure what had held our attackers back, and whatever it was couldn't last forever.

I tried to pick up my pace as I passed the vampires, but my body wouldn't cooperate. Stress, fighting, and injuries had taken their toll. The ground underneath me seemed to shift like there was an earthquake, but no one else seemed panicked.

If the shadows caught up with us now, I wasn't sure I could fight them off. Whatever had happened back there to make them withdraw had been a gift from Fate, which made me nervous.

The bitch had never liked me—she had to be setting me up for an even worse scenario.

Keeping to a quick jog instead of the run I wanted, I continued toward the vehicle. The panting of Gage,

Xander, and Kendric and the sounds of Briar's footsteps drove me forward. We were making progress, and I needed to focus on that.

My shifter hearing perked up when I heard Raven clear her throat. "If you want to have a conversation about what duties you three are in charge of and what decisions I can make, now isn't the time to discuss that, seeing as we both agree that you all need to remain here. We should take that up later, upon your return to the mansion, so we can include the queen herself in the conversation to ensure there are no misunderstandings on any of our parts. Wouldn't you agree?"

Despite the exhaustion weighing down my body, I felt the corners of my lips turn slightly upward. Martin had intended to use his authority to put Raven in her place and embarrass her in front of the guards, but she had stood her ground firmly. Maybe it wasn't just alpha wolf-shifter men who had the problem—maybe small-dick syndrome was an issue with men of all species.

There was a long pause until Bella huffed. "Fine. Until then, the three of us need to handle this situation."

I wanted to roll my eyes, but I didn't have the energy to spare, so I just kept moving forward.

A few minutes later, Raven caught up and kept pace beside me. I expected her to speak, but she didn't. We ran through some trees running parallel with the road that formed the border between the territory of the Shae lands and the state park, which meant the vehicles were less than two hundred yards away, hidden by thick trees and brush.

I glanced at her and asked, "Is there something you want to say?"

She took a quick breath. "No. Why?"

"You can run a lot faster than I can, so I figured there's a reason you're staying behind with me." Especially when Kendric was ahead of me, carrying Ryker.

She snorted, not sounding half the lady she appeared to be. "You won't like the answer, so it's probably best if I don't tell you." She arched a perfectly sculpted eyebrow.

Disappointment made me falter. "You don't trust me." My wolf whimpered and snarled within.

We'd spent a decent amount of time together while I'd focused on Briar's and my pack bond to locate my sister's general vicinity before the alpha meeting the Blackwoods had called. We'd wanted to show up and shock them enough to trick whoever was holding Briar into giving himself away, and we'd accomplished that. I'd thought Raven and I had established some goodwill between us. Clearly, it had been one-sided.

"What?" Her jaw dropped as we made our way through the woods. "That's not it at all. You look as if you could crash at any second, and I don't want you to get any more injured than you already are."

My head spun. I didn't know whether to thank her or placate my wolf by telling Raven we were fine, so I did the worst possible thing and remained silent.

The oaks and pines around us thinned out, revealing the black SUV Ryker and I had driven here. The three cars the vampires had loaned Gage, Xander, and Kendric also sat untouched. They'd taken separate cars so they could scout out the three packs in this area and determine who was holding my sister. Of course it had been the pack that I'd least expected...one that my pack had spent time with occasionally.

Briar leaned against the black Ford Charger, taking deep breaths as Kendric and Xander lay on their bellies, keeping Ryker on their backs. I quickly noticed that one person was missing. "Where's Gage?"

"I think he went to shift." Briar gestured toward a sizable oak tree about fifty yards away.

As if Gage had timed it perfectly, he stepped around the tree in human form, dressed in a black shirt and jeans. "I figured we all need to shift to drive these vehicles back to the mansion."

He was right. We couldn't leave the cars here in case humans stumbled upon them. No vehicles were allowed off-road in the woods. The last thing we needed was human park rangers knocking on the door of a gigantic mansion full of vampires and asking questions.

But first things first. "I can drive the SUV. Let's get Ryker in so we can get him some help."

I jogged to the black Suburban and opened the back door.

"Uh, no. You won't be driving." Raven shook her head and moved to one side of Ryker. "You're injured and lost a lot of blood."

"She's right." Briar straightened as if trying to appear strong. "I'll drive it."

"You don't know where the mansion is, and you've been held captive for over a week." Raven karate-chopped the air. "I'll be the one driving. Gage, I need you to help me get Ryker into the back seat, and then Briar can help Ember take care of him. Ember, recline the mid-row seat behind the driver's back, and we can lay him down so he doesn't fall over when we bring him to you."

Equal parts gratitude and the desire to be the only one helping Ryker shot through me. I chose to focus on the part that meant I didn't drop him and make his injuries worse. I did as she asked, climbing in and lowering the seatbacks even as my own back convulsed in agony.

In unison, Kendric and Xander stood and carried Ryker over to me with Raven on his uninjured side and Gage on the side with the knife. When they reached the door, I scooted back to guide Ryker in as the two of them worked together to lay him down in the seat.

As soon as Ryker was safely settled, Kendric and Xander ran off toward the trees, no doubt to shift and grab the clothes they'd surely stashed there when they'd met up to scout out the area together.

In the sudden quiet, I could hear Ryker's vitals clearly. My heart crashed into my stomach.

His heartbeat was slowing.

# CHAPTER FOUR

A crushing weight seemed to fall on my chest, making it impossible to breathe. How could the thought of this man—whom I had once despised almost as much as Reid—dying make me want to scream?

I hadn't realized how much I'd grown to care for him. For the last four days, he'd protected me and taken care of me while I was on the mend. I had a hard time associating him with the man who'd tortured Simon maliciously—the man who'd pulled me from the river so I wouldn't drown but who'd planned on leaving me on the embankment to die slowly, and the man whom I'd heard had beaten others needlessly.

That same man had jumped in front of a knife to protect my sister. Now I owed him a life debt that I needed to pay sooner than I'd ever expected.

"Raven, we gotta go," I said, voice thick from desperation. "We need to stop the bleeding, or we're going to lose him."

The skin around her eyes tightened as she vanished from her spot next to Gage, and the front driver's side door quickly opened and closed. The top of her head appeared in front of Ryker. She started the SUV just as Briar rushed to the front passenger door.

Gage took a step back, his lips pressed into a line. "We'll catch up. Go to the mansion, and we'll meet you there." He slammed the door.

Not even the loud *bang* startled Ryker.

A salty-sour taste filled my mouth as my stomach roiled. With every second, the situation seemed to grow more and more dire.

The problem was that the mansion was an hour away, and I was certain Ryker didn't have that long. However, we couldn't take him to a hospital, and there wasn't a pack we could trust. The Shae pack was under attack, even if I had thought we could take him to them. "We're not going to be able to wait to get to the mansion."

Raven dodged a tree and glanced over her shoulder. "Where did the knife stab him?"

"His side. He jumped in front of our attacker just as whatever it was tried to stab Briar," I gritted out, trying like hell to keep my voice neutral.

The SUV hit a bump, and then Raven peeled out of the woods and onto solid asphalt.

Briar yelped from her spot in front as Ryker's body jerked toward me. I caught him with both hands and dropped to my knees in the small opening between our two seats, not wanting the knife to cause further problems.

Pain exploded in my back, and my knees ached. I bit back a whimper, knowing that Raven was trying to get us back to the mansion as quickly as possible.

Briar whipped her head toward me, forehead lined. "Are you okay?" Her anger and disgust from earlier seemed completely gone.

"I'll be fine." The last person anyone needed to worry about at this moment was me. Ryker would die if we didn't do something quickly.

Biting the inside of my cheek so I didn't make any noises of pain, I kept one hand on his chest and moved so I could see where the knife went in.

His shirt and pants were soaked in blood, and the coppery smell had me ready to gag. I swallowed hard and tried to gently rip the rest of his shirt so I could see as much of the wound as possible.

Warm blood wetted my fingertips once more, softening the congealed blood on my hand. My wolf whimpered inside me in both hurt and rage at what had been done to Ryker.

I wanted to embrace the emotions, but I couldn't. Not right now. I didn't have the time or luxury to be anything but calm and rational in this moment.

I leaned forward, the smell of blood so strong now I could taste iron on my tongue. I held my breath and leaned closer, my nose nearly touching Ryker's blood-soaked shirt as I tried to get a better look.

The knife protruded from between his ribs at a sharp upward angle, the blade disappearing into his flesh. The skin around the entry point was inflamed. Blood oozed steadily from the wound, trickling down Ryker's side and pooling on the seat beneath him.

With trembling fingers, I gently touched the skin around the knife, and a buzz shot up my arm like wildfire. I never knew when I would feel this strange connection between us, but when the sensation did come, it was both pleasant and unwanted.

Right now, I'd take it because it was confirmation that he was going to live... At least, I'd embrace that delusion to get through this.

Relieved that he hadn't reacted negatively to my touch, I moved closer to the wound, noticing his skin became warmer the closer I got to the entry point.

My heart dropped into my stomach. Was the warmth a good sign or a bad one? Either way, I had to do the best I could with what we had. I continued to palpate the area near the blade.

Ryker winced, and his muscles turned rigid then twitched.

I jerked my hand back. Had I hurt him? I swallowed hard, my throat tight with worry. "Raven, the dagger went in at an angle between his ribs. It's not a straight stab wound."

Raven exhaled loudly. "That's actually good news." Her voice sounded less strained. "Based on the angle and what I can hear, it doesn't sound like it hit any major arteries. The blood loss isn't as rapid or forceful as it would be with arterial damage."

A little bit of relief washed over me, but he'd still lost too much blood. "Should I try to put pressure on the wound to make the bleeding stop?"

Raven met my gaze in the rearview mirror, her usually warm cognac eyes dark with worry and fear. "It'd be best to remove the knife so we can truly put pressure on the wound to clot the whole thing. Leaving it in risks further damage, especially if it shifts and prolongs the bleeding. We need the entire wound to clot, and you need to remove it while he still has enough strength for his wolf magic to help heal him."

My stomach dropped at the thought of pulling out the blade. I'd seen plenty of movies and TV shows, and they always said to leave the knife in. But Raven was centuries old and had no doubt dealt with countless injuries during her long life. If she thought removing it was best, I had to trust her judgment. She hadn't steered us wrong yet; in fact, she'd been our best ally.

Briar turned around in her seat, her expression twisted with fear and uncertainty. "Are you sure we should remove the knife?" Her voice trembled. "What if it makes him bleed out faster? We have to think this through. This man sacrificed himself for me. If something goes wrong..."

The weight of Briar's worries pressed on me as I tried to keep up a steady facade. Deep down, my stomach fluttered, and it wasn't from warm feelings. Was Raven really making the right call? Would I regret trusting her in this life-and-death situation?

Still, doing *nothing* wasn't an option, and Raven's logic made sense. Regardless, the decision had to be made quickly. I wasn't sure if I was ready for the consequences, but waiting wasn't a luxury I had.

I took a deep breath, steeling myself. We had no better choice. Every second that ticked by was another drop of blood Ryker couldn't afford to lose.

"I'm going to do it," I said, my voice steadier than I felt inside. "With the blade left inside, he'll continue to bleed, and his heart is getting weaker."

Briar's eyes widened, a mix of what seemed to be fear and doubt clouding her gaze. In less than an hour, we'd broken her out of a makeshift prison, been attacked by enemies no one but I could see, and now I was asking her to trust a vampire, a member of the one species wolves inherently didn't get along with because vampire magic came from taking life—blood—which clashed with how wolf magic connected with nature and helped maintain balance.

I didn't want to upset Briar more, but I did believe that

removing the knife was our best bet. I gritted my teeth, hating that I was about to cause Ryker more pain but knowing it was necessary to save his life.

I leaned over Ryker to reach the wound. Taking a deep breath, I grasped the hilt firmly with both hands. The cool metal contrasted sharply with the warm, sticky blood coating Ryker's skin and my hands.

As soon as my fingers wrapped around the handle, Ryker let out a low, pained groan. His body tensed, his muscles going rigid beneath my touch. I froze, my heart racing as I looked at his face. His eyes remained closed, but his brows furrowed, emphasizing the scar down the middle of his left one.

My chest constricted as I inhaled shakily. "I'm sorry," I whispered, though I wasn't sure Ryker could even hear me in his unconscious state.

With one swift movement, I yanked the blade from Ryker's side. His eyes snapped open, and an anguished scream erupted from his throat. He thrashed against the seat, muscles bulging under his taut skin. More blood seeped from the wound.

"Briar, help me restrain him!" I yelled, tossing the bloodstained knife to the floorboard. I climbed over his waist, straddling him.

I pressed my weight down to try to keep him still as he continued to thrash. His muscles rippled beneath me, and if he'd been in full health, he would've easily thrown me off. I placed my hands on his broad shoulders, feeling the heat of his skin through his blood-soaked shirt and the faint buzz that sparked when we touched.

Briar scrambled over the center console and reached around me to hold down his hands. But as soon as she touched him, he fought her off, causing even more bleeding.

"Ryker, it's me. Ember." I leaned forward, trying to make him focus on my face. "You're safe. We had to remove the knife."

His wild eyes locked with mine. The sheen that sometimes covered them was gone, revealing their gorgeous brown color. The gold could barely be seen.

Then the gold sparked, and his expression softened. The corners of his mouth tipped upward slightly. "Em...ber," he rasped. "I was...worried. You're...safe."

My heart skipped a beat.

His hand trembled as he raised it and touched my cheek, leaving a warm wetness behind. A smudge of blood, I assumed.

My throat closed, and something sweetly painful unfurled in my chest. It almost seemed as if Ryker...cared about me.

I exhaled and shook off that thought. If Reid—my fated mate—could turn on me, Ryker definitely could. I wouldn't leave him and the others until I knew they were safe and accounted for, but the more time I spent with him—with all of them—the harder it would be to leave. And I had to leave for both Briar's and my safety.

But when Ryker's hand fell limply to his side, my heart plummeted. His eyes fluttered closed, and his breathing grew shallow and ragged.

"No, no, no!" My voice rose in panic. "Ryker, stay with me!"

He was no longer fighting us, so I was able to move my hands to his wound and press firmly against it.

Warm blood continued to seep between my fingers at an alarming rate. The metallic scent of copper filled the air, making my stomach churn.

"Oh Fate, Ember," Briar gasped, moving to the mid-row

seat I'd been sitting in. "It's bleeding so much more now. I told you it wasn't smart to remove it!"

Doubt crept into my mind. Had I made the wrong choice? The blood continued to ooze steadily between my fingers. Each trickle felt like another grain of sand slipping through an hourglass, counting down the precious seconds of Ryker's life.

His skin grew paler, and his heartbeat weakened further. Panic clawed at my chest. I pressed harder against the wound, desperate enough to beg Fate to help me. *Please, please, please.* If he died because I'd made the wrong decision, I wasn't sure I'd be able to live with it.

"Don't listen to her, Ember. Leaving it in would have been even worse," Raven said confidently. "The knife could have shifted and caused more harm. This is the best chance to stop the bleeding since the blade missed an artery. There's no gushing sound, which would indicate we made the wrong call. And right now, doubt is your enemy. You need to focus on saving him."

As Raven's words sank in, I forced myself to take a deep breath and refocus. She was right—doubt would only hinder me. The decision had been made, and I had to continue with the plan.

Desperate to slow the bleeding, I pressed my hands against the gaping wound. I glanced around, searching for something to use to help clot the injury.

The strange sensation flared inside me, warmth pulsing from my chest and flowing into my hands. It seemed to connect with something primal and hot, reminding me of my wolf magic.

I shook my head, trying to dispel the weird feeling. Between the grief of losing my pack, the stress of our current situation, and the bizarre shadows only I could see,

I'd begun to question my own sanity. These odd feelings and sensations had to be my mind playing tricks on me. And I couldn't afford to get distracted now.

Ignoring the strange warmth, I surveyed the SUV again for anything I could use to help stop the bleeding. The leather seats and floor were already slick with Ryker's blood, and I didn't see a damn thing that would be better to use than my hands.

I looked down at my own bloodstained shirt. The fabric was torn and dirty from the earlier fight, but it was still better than nothing.

The SUV hit another bump, jostling us. Ryker's body shifted beneath me. I waited for the blood to pour, but despite the tingles in my hands, I didn't feel any pulse of fresh blood.

I removed my hands and grabbed the hem of my shirt.

"What are you doing?" Briar cried and leaned toward me. "You can't stop putting pressure on it."

"I need something to help clot the wound." I removed my shirt and winced as my damaged back burned with the movement. "My hands alone aren't enough."

Cool air hit my bare torso, and I bundled up the shirt, keeping the cleanest portion outside to press against his injury.

My eyes flicked back to Ryker's rib cage, and I blinked several times, trying to understand what I was seeing.

# CHAPTER FIVE

No matter what I did, each time I opened my eyes, I saw the same thing. I struggled to make sense of it because, even in the supernatural world, healing this rapidly was unheard of.

Moments ago, Ryker's wound had been gaping and bleeding alarmingly. If I didn't know any better, I would swear this wasn't the same injury.

The skin around the stab wound was pink and puckered, as if a day's worth of shifter healing had happened in mere minutes. The flow of blood had ceased entirely, leaving behind only the congealed evidence that it had been bleeding as horribly as I remembered.

Seeing my reaction, Briar's brows furrowed. "What's wrong?" She leaned over toward Ryker's injury.

My lungs stopped working. The urge to grip her by the nape of the neck and yank her away from him had my spine straightening. Forcing air out of my lungs, I attempted to keep a level head. After all, Briar was my sister, and she felt responsible for Ryker's injuries because they'd happened while he was protecting *her*.

She gasped and recoiled. Her jaw dropped open for a moment before she muttered, "How is that even possible?"

With trembling hands, she reached toward him, and my heart raced.

All sense of calm vanished. Before she could touch him, my possessive instincts took over, and I smacked her hand away.

I almost snapped, *Don't touch him. He belongs to me!* But somehow, I managed to keep my lips sealed.

Briar's gaze jerked in my direction. Her eyes widened as she placed her hand back in her lap. "What the hell? Why did you do that?"

"What's going on back there?" Raven asked, her voice tense. "I still hear his heart beating, so you need to tell me what's wrong."

I rubbed my hands together, feeling gooeyness from the blood caked on them. The fierce protectiveness I'd felt moments ago began to ebb, replaced by a lump of confusion and guilt in my throat. I struggled to find words to explain myself, knowing I couldn't reveal the possessive thoughts that had raced through my mind.

"I—I'm sorry," I stammered, forcing myself to maintain eye contact with her so I didn't come off even more peculiar. "We don't know if there was anything on the blade, so it's best if you don't touch the wound, just in case."

Briar's eyes narrowed, but she nodded. "That makes sense, but why the hell did *you* touch the wound then? Your life is more important than mine."

A wave of guilt crashed over me. I struggled to find the right words to explain my actions. While my excuse might make logical sense, I hadn't even considered it until I'd wanted to hide the reason for my gut reaction.

She was right. If the blade had been poisoned or

magicked, I could have been infected. "I didn't think about it until just now. I wasn't trying to put myself at risk, but Briar, I'll do anything to protect you. My life isn't more important than yours, and I never want to hear you say that again." I *was* protecting her now, even from myself, since my gut reaction had been to inflict pain on her so that she never wanted to touch Ryker again.

I couldn't believe the powerful possessive instinct that had surged through me, even toward Briar.

Inhaling through my mouth, I tasted the strong copper scent. It mixed with the salty, sour taste on my tongue. My heart seized inside my chest with so much pain and worry over Ryker.

He had become a distraction. One I couldn't afford and had to get away from. Briar's safety was all that mattered now. I couldn't afford to worry about strange feelings or impossible healing, and I especially couldn't give another man the power to hurt and humiliate me. I'd made that mistake once, and I refused to do it ever again.

Which meant I had only one choice. "Once we know Ryker is safe, we need to get you away from all this. We need to leave and start fresh somewhere away from here. Somewhere the shadows can't find us."

She bit her bottom lip. "But where else can we go? We have no pack, no home."

Her words hung heavy in the air, the brutal truth of our situation hitting me like a punch to the gut. How could I keep Briar safe when I couldn't even trust my own instincts?

I gazed out the window at the blur of trees rushing past, searching for answers in the shadowy landscape. The forest seemed to mock us with its vastness, offering a thousand hiding places and just as many dangers. Moonlight filtered through the branches, casting eerie shadows that danced and twisted, reminding me of the iridescent attackers only I could see.

"I'm using my centuries' worth of patience right now, but it's running low," Raven said, steering the vehicle on the curvy road. "What's going on with Ryker? I've only been able to stay quiet this long because I don't hear blood like I could before. Were you able to clot it?"

My focus landed back on Ryker's wound, and I could suddenly feel the floorboard biting into my knees. "I...I don't even know how to explain it." I filled her in. Shifter healing was quick and amazing, but he'd been so injured that it hadn't done anything until I'd removed the knife.

Raven remained silent for a long moment. The SUV swayed as we took another curve, and I braced my hands on the sides of Ryker's seat, trying not to fall on or jostle him.

Finally, she sighed and replied, "The knife must have prevented the progress. Removing it allowed his wolf to heal him. He's from the strongest line of wolves now since the royals have passed, which means he should heal more quickly than an average shifter."

The pieces clicked into place, and some of my bewilderment eased from my chest. I'd felt warmth when I'd touched Ryker's wound with my bare hands, which shouldn't have been possible, but I'd recognized an animalistic magic that felt very similar to mine. "That makes sense. I'm glad he was still strong enough to heal himself." Fate only knew what would've happened if he hadn't been.

The three of us fell into silence, with only the sounds of the engine and Ryker's heartbeat to accompany the journey.

Briar sagged back into the seat with a deep exhale of relief. She leaned. "Thank goodness," she breathed. "I don't know what I would have done if he... If he hadn't made it."

She ran a hand through her greasy, matted copper hair. "He saved my life. I owe him *everything*."

"That's an interesting choice of words, especially since Ember doesn't feel the same way." I could hear Raven fidgeting behind me, my back still to the driver's seat. "To say I'm disappointed would be an understatement."

A knot formed tightly in my stomach. With her vampire ears, there was no question that she'd heard me tell Briar we needed to leave, but I had to push past the guilt. No matter what, Briar was my top priority.

"What do you mean?" Briar tilted her head and squinted at me.

I opened my mouth to attempt to mitigate the situation, but Raven continued before I could speak. "Ember mentioned leaving the mansion once we arrive. I'm curious about this plan, especially given the current situation."

I swallowed hard, guilt constricting my throat. Raven's words weren't accusing but rather disappointed, which made them sting even worse. I couldn't deny that she was right. After everything Ryker, his pack, and the vampires had done for us, leaving felt like a betrayal. But the memory of Reid's public rejection still burned, a constant reminder of why I couldn't let my guard down again.

"I..." My voice cracked, and I cleared my throat. "I appreciate everything you've done for us, but Briar's safety has to be my top priority."

As if on cue, Ryker let out a low, pained groan. His eyelids fluttered and his muscles tensed. I was acutely aware of every movement he made. I leaned over him, checking his wound to make sure it hadn't started bleeding again.

His face pinched. His chest rose and fell with shallow, labored breaths. I leaned closer, my own pulse thudding as I searched for any signs that might hint he wasn't as well off as I had hoped.

"Ember," he croaked.

Somehow, him saying my name a second time sent an even stronger shiver along my back. His eyes, usually so sharp and alert, were clouded with pain and exhaustion. Yet, as they focused on my face, the golden flecks warmed, and my breath caught.

"I'm here." I forced a smile, desperate to reassure him. "How are you feeling?"

Ryker snorted and then groaned. "Like I've been stabbed," he managed with a hint of his usual humor.

Knowing he needed me to act normal, I tried to play it cool. But my wolf stirred inside, wanting to comfort him, to touch him, and to make sure he really was okay.

Despite the pain etched on his face, his eyes never left mine. The air between us seemed to crackle with the familiar cadence of the buzz that sprang up between us when we touched.

"Well, you're looking better than you did just five minutes ago." I forced my tone to be light and to hide the terror that had been brewing inside. "Your healing kicked in pretty impressively once we got that knife out."

His lips twitched. "Perks of being a strong wolf of the royal guard, I suppose."

Briar sniffed, bringing me back to the present. For a moment, it had felt like Ryker and I were the only two beings in the world. Now my sister fidgeted, turning her whole body toward him. "Thank you so much for saving me." Emotion deepened her voice. "I can't believe you risked your life like that for someone you barely know."

He looked at her, his expression softening. "There's no need to thank me," he said. He shifted slightly and winced.

"I'm the alpha of the Grimstone pack. Protecting our species is my job." He looked at me, his expression softening. The faint glow in his eyes indicated his wolf had inched forward. "And some people are worth protecting at any cost."

The meaning of his words was clear—he'd done it for me. He didn't have to say it outright because I understood him better than I wanted to admit. Still, my heart raced, and every time I tried to move my gaze, I couldn't. My wolf snarled, and I couldn't even force myself to turn my head.

*Is there something you need to share with me?* Briar linked, and our connection thrummed with curiosity.

My mind raced, trying to find the right words to explain something I barely understood myself...something that I needed to forget about and put behind me. *There's nothing to share.* I flinched as the sulfur scent of a lie filled the vehicle. My wolf growled inside, letting me know she was pissed that I wouldn't acknowledge how I felt about Ryker.

I wanted to chastise her, but I had something more important to focus on.

*Everyone in here can smell that big fat lie you just told.* Briar arched a brow and crossed her arms.

Fate being the bitch she was, Ryker coughed then flinched and groaned. "Either someone just lied, or their stomach is upset." His eyelids sagged as he turned his head toward both Briar and me.

"Definitely a lie," Raven replied. "I have a feeling I know exactly what it's about, too."

*Spill it.* Briar pursed her lips, which was her tell that she was determined about something. She didn't get like this often, but clearly, Ryker had made a huge impression on her by nearly dying to save her.

I exhaled, knowing that I couldn't get out of this. But

that didn't mean I had to tell her everything. I didn't even understand my feelings for him, so how could I explain them? The pull I felt toward him shouldn't be possible, and the fear that gripped my heart at the thought of trusting anyone again after Reid's betrayal was strong. Not only that, but the best way to protect Briar was to get her as far away from here as possible.

*It's...complicated.* I shrugged, and my mouth dried.

I tilted my head back, looking at the gray ceiling. I didn't want to see her expression as I linked my next words. *I can't explain our connection.* Even though I didn't say it out loud, my tongue felt dry and fat. *I don't fully understand it myself. But I do know that Reid's rejection destroyed my world and future, and I refuse to let myself be that vulnerable again.* I pushed away the warmth that bloomed in my chest. *Besides, the Blackwoods clearly want us dead, so we can't stay around here. It's not safe.*

I rolled my shoulders and focused on Ryker again. My heart clenched at the sight of his pale face. His eyes were closed once more, and his breathing evened out as he slipped back into unconsciousness.

*Ember, it's not safe anywhere for us right now.* Briar shook her head and wrinkled her nose. *You want to leave our friends from our neighboring packs as if they're nothing.*

Her words stung, but I couldn't let them sway me. I had to stay focused on our survival. *Our* friends? I let the heat of my anger float through our connection. *What friends, Briar? The ones who slaughtered our pack after their alpha heir rejected me in front of everyone? The ones who tried to kill us again tonight? None of the other packs came to our defense either, not even during the alpha meeting I attended to determine who might be holding you captive!*

She winced, but I pressed on, unable to stop now that

the floodgates had opened. *And now you want to stay here after you got upset with me for allying with the Grimstones to find you and because we're heading back to the royal vampire nest? Do you not remember all the stories we heard from Dad about the Grimstones growing up, how they don't hesitate to torture people? Because I can tell you, it's true. I watched Ryker beat up someone innocent, trying to get answers.* In fairness, with my growing rage, I understood Ryker more—another reason I needed to get away. I didn't want hate to consume me like it had him.

Her nostrils flared. *I understand what happened, but none of the other packs had time to get there to help us. How could they expect something like that to happen when we didn't? Ryker nearly died protecting me. And now you want to run away before we even make sure he's recovered?*

My back stiffened. *I'm trying to keep us alive, Briar. We can't trust* anyone *right now. They could turn on us at any second.*

*So what's your plan then? Are we wandering off into the wilderness alone, with no allies and no resources, hoping the Blackwoods don't find us?*

*I plan on relocating us to the West Coast. Yeah, we'll be starting over, and it'll be hard, but it's better than staying here waiting to be massacred.* I gritted my teeth, trying to remain calm.

Briar lifted her chin. *You may believe that, but I don't. I won't run.*

There had been only a handful of times that Briar had stood her ground. But after losing our entire pack, I'd never imagined this would be one of them. *You're going. End of discussion.*

*No. I'm not willing. You alpha-willed me earlier to make me leave you behind. You'll have to take away another of my choices to make this happen.* She clenched her jaw. *Something I will* never *forgive you for, Ember. I want to make that clear.*

My wolf snarled, disliking her talking back to us. If alpha-willing was what it took, then I guessed it was time. I'd rather have her alive to hate me than have to bury her.

I tugged at my wolf, preparing to lose my sister forever.

# CHAPTER SIX

Inhaling deeply, I gathered myself and prepared to force Briar to obey me. The warm, animalistic surge of alpha power coursed through my veins, prickling beneath my skin. I set my jaw and locked my focus on my sister, making sure to unleash the full force of my will.

But as I opened my mouth to speak, I froze. The look on her face stopped me cold, and my words died in my throat.

She lifted her chin higher in stubborn determination. Her eyes, usually so warm and full of life, now blazed with a fierce defiance I'd never seen before. There was something more to them—they held a darkness, a mixture of hurt, betrayal, and disgust, that pierced my heart.

At that moment, I saw not only my little sister, but a reflection of myself from over a week ago, standing before Reid Blackwood.

Her look mirrored how I'd felt standing before him the day my world had shattered.

I recalled the mix of emotions that had coursed through me—the hurt, the betrayal, the crushing weight of humiliation. But most of all, I remembered the helplessness and the way he hadn't seemed to care how I felt. The experience of having my choices stripped away, of being at the mercy of someone else's decision about my life and future.

Realization crashed over me, taking my breath away. I was about to do to my own sister exactly what Reid had done to me. The very reason I wanted to protect her and get away from everything.

I would have used my power to force her down a path she didn't want and, more importantly, a path she didn't agree with in the slightest.

The alpha power drained from me, leaving me hollow and shaken. My legs felt weak, and I collapsed against the back of the driver's seat, my butt hitting the floorboard.

My chest tightened as I stared at Briar, seeing her not just as my little sister but as a woman who had endured unimaginable trauma and loss. The fierce cut of her features spoke volumes about the strength she'd found within herself.

"Briar, I..." My voice cracked, thick with emotion. I swallowed hard while my eyes burned and grew blurry with unshed tears. "I'm so sorry. I won't do it. I won't force you to leave."

The hard lines of worry eased from her face, and she dropped her chin an inch. But the skin around her eyes remained tight, a reminder of the trust between us that I'd nearly broken but still harmed.

I took a shaky breath, the words tumbling out in a rush. "When Reid rejected me, I didn't just lose my fated mate. I lost everything I thought my future would be and what our parents wanted for me. My place in the pack, my role as an alpha heir's mate and future beta, the family I'd dreamed of having... In an instant, it all crumbled, and all of our supposed *friends* stood by and watched it happen. It wasn't just Reid who abandoned me; it was everyone we considered a friend who didn't speak up that day. But the absolute worst part was feeling like I had no control, no say in what happened to me.

"I felt so helpless, so powerless. Like the life I'd expected to have just...vanished before me, with no consideration for my wants and needs. And I almost did the exact same thing to you."

Her expression softened, and she pursed her lips. "So you understand why I can't just run away? Why I need to make my own choice about this?"

I nodded, shame and guilt churning in my stomach. "I do understand. I was so focused on protecting you that I almost became the very thing I was trying to shield you from. I'm so sorry, Briar."

Silence filled the vehicle until Raven snorted. "Well, isn't that touching? Ember learned she couldn't trust her friends, so she decided to do the exact same thing to Ryker and the rest of us. Because clearly, the best way to deal with betrayal is to become the betrayer yourself."

My head jerked back. Her words stung, but I couldn't deny the truth in them. I had been ready to abandon the very people who risked everything to help us. But the other packs, including Reid's, *had* helped our pack before that fateful day. "I can't handle being treated like that again and losing more people I care about." And worse, if Ryker lost interest in me or found his fated mate... I didn't want to hang around and witness *that*.

Ryker's face had relaxed. He was still unconscious, but his heartbeat had strengthened, which meant he was healthier.

Even in sleep, there was a strength to his features—the sharp line of his jaw and the scar that marked his left eyebrow somehow made him look even more ruggedly handsome. His dark lashes rested against his cheeks, and a lock of his dark hair had fallen across his forehead.

My fingers itched to brush it back. His lips, usually set in a hard line, were softened now. I remembered the way they'd felt on mine when he'd kissed me at the alpha meeting.

My chest warmed.

I shook my head, trying to push those thoughts away. Even if we stayed, I couldn't get more attached to him. That would be my ultimate downfall.

Raven's dry laughter startled me.

"You foolish, naive girl. Do you really think running away will protect you from pain? From loss?" Her voice gentled, taking on an almost wistful tone. "I've lived for centuries. I've seen alliances form and deteriorate, watched countless lovers come together and then break each other's hearts. And let me tell you, there is no escaping the ache of loss, no matter what you do. Severing all relationships will only leave you lonely, which is a whole different kind of hurt. Pain is as much a part of life as blood running through your veins."

But that was the thing—I wouldn't be alone. "All I need is Briar."

"You think you're protecting yourself by leaving? By cutting ties yourself before they can be severed by another? All you're doing is denying yourself the chance to truly live." Raven released a long sigh. "Not only that, but it's clear that Briar wants relationships with others."

I huffed and closed my eyes for a moment. I hadn't considered that which was ridiculous in retrospect. When I opened them once again, Briar nodded.

"I love you, but I want to have a mate and family." Briar

lifted both hands and warmth flooded back into her eyes. "Reid's rejection, the loss of our pack, and us being separated are all still so fresh. You'll change your mind when you have time to heal."

Suddenly, I felt as if I were submerged under water, and my lungs burned like I couldn't breathe. I couldn't fathom changing my mind, and yet, I'd have to. Briar desired a family. That was something that I couldn't keep from her unless I constantly alpha-willed her, and what kind of relationship would we have if I did that?

"Ember, you have to understand that closing yourself off isn't living; it's merely existing. I've watched countless humans over the centuries, seen how fleeting and fragile their connections can be. If you go somewhere and surround yourselves with humans, you're even more likely to be betrayed. Supernaturals have the capacity for so much more connection. Our bonds run deeper; our loyalties, fiercer."

I rolled my shoulders and got my feet under me. I didn't want to be examined like a lab specimen. As I stood a little, my legs buckled, indicating that I'd been squatting too long. I sat in the space between the mid-row seats and stretched out my legs, feeling Briar's gaze on me the entire time.

Raven continued, "I've seen packs torn apart by betrayal, but I've also witnessed unwavering loyalty when they had a shared hardship. I've watched vampires who were once bitter enemies become the closest of allies over centuries. There's a depth to supernatural relationships that humans can rarely fathom."

From my spot, I could see Raven's face in the rearview mirror. Her expression was strained, and black strands of hair framed her face, making her features appear sharper.

I wanted to plug my ears, but that would be childish

and stupid. Pointless too—I'd still be able to hear her with my supernatural hearing.

"Think about it, Ember." She glanced in the mirror, our gazes connecting. "In a human lifetime, how many true, deep connections can one form, given how quickly they age and the hardships they face without magic? The subconscious feeling of being prey, without understanding that it causes so much turmoil in their lives, to the point where they lash out at one another. We supernaturals have the potential for so much more. We are the top of the food chain and can forge bonds that last centuries, weathering storms that would break lesser relationships."

I closed my eyes, trying to block out her words, but memories of the past flashed through my mind.

The warmth of my mother's embrace as she comforted me as a child after a nightmare, her familiar scent of lavender and pine wrapping around me like her strong arms. The pride in my father's eyes as he watched me shift without any issues for the first time. The uncontrollable laughter shared with Briar as we splashed in the crystal-clear river that had almost caused our deaths, our giggles echoing through the woods.

Then came more recent memories: Ryker's strong arms carrying me after I was attacked by a vampire, his touch sending sparks through my body. The fierce protectiveness in his eyes as he jumped in front of the knife to protect my sister.

As Raven's words hit me like a ton of bricks, my face warmed with embarrassment and guilt. Briar turned in her seat to look at me, so I averted my gaze to the floorboard between the middle seats. I needed a moment to process my emotions and couldn't do that while locking eyes with her.

"I didn't realize you were struggling so much," Briar said

quietly. "About what happened with Reid. The betrayal and hurt you experienced. You always take things in stride and rarely show weakness, so I had no clue how much it impacted you. I'm so sorry I wasn't there for you more."

My head snapped up. "Don't you dare apologize." I placed a hand over my heart. "I wanted to handle it alone. You weren't responsible for helping me overcome that."

"Why do you always do that?" Briar frowned. "You never want my help, yet you're the first person I come to when I need someone."

Was that even a serious question? "Because I'm your big sister, and it's my responsibility to protect you from everything...even myself."

Hurt shadowed her eyes, and disappointment etched into her features. "I'm not a kid anymore, Ember. I want you to rely on me too, instead of telling me what to do and forcing your will on me."

My heart dropped into my stomach. I'd somehow made the situation even worse. "I... I'm so sorry," I choked. "To both of you. Briar, of course I rely on you, but I wasn't in the right head space to talk about it. I'm just now getting to that point. I didn't mean to make it seem like I don't value your opinion or want you to be there for me. Your warmth is one of the qualities I admire most about you, and it's why you're putting your foot down with me now for wanting to leave the very people who risked their lives to save you."

She opened her mouth to respond, but I lifted a finger because I needed to get it all out before I let something that needed to be said slip from my mind. "I never want you to resent me. I was so focused on keeping you safe that I lost sight of what really matters—your happiness and freedom to choose your own path."

The last bit of disappointment and anger vanished from

her face as she reached for me, placing her hand on my still-numb leg.

Her eyes glistened. "I know. That's why I argued with you—because there's no doubt in my mind how much you love and care for me. You're an amazingly strong person, and I do trust you with both my emotional and physical safety."

Between her validation and Ryker improving each minute, my lungs began working normally once more, and I took a deep breath. "And I do the same with you." Her wolf might not be as strong as mine, but she loved more fiercely than I ever could.

Unfortunately, I wasn't done yet. "Raven, I didn't mean to be ungrateful. If you all hadn't shown up tonight, there's no way the six of us would've gotten away. You and Queen Ambrosia gave us the resources to remain safe while I focused on locating Briar, and then you gave us the vehicles that helped us get Briar back. To be clear, I didn't want to abandon you." I let out a shaky breath, hating that I'd almost done to them what I resented other packs for doing to us. "I didn't think of it that way—I was focused on protecting the only family and pack member I have left."

Raven pressed her lips into a line, her expression shifting from hurt to understanding. "I know, Ember. Believe me, I understand the desperate need to protect those you love. When you've lived as long as I have, you learn that the pain of loss never truly fades. It's a constant companion, whispering in your ear at random times or during quiet moments. The pain can suffocate me unexpectedly."

She leaned her head back against the headrest and turned into the paved driveway. "But that same pain is what makes the connections we forge so precious. It's the price we pay for allowing ourselves to care and love. And that's the only thing that has gotten me through at times, especially right now when there's so much at stake."

I grimaced, remembering that she'd just lost someone she cared deeply for in the recent nest eradication. Kendric had been distraught over telling her about it.

Silence filled the vehicle. I flexed my ankles, the needle pricks subsiding now that blood flow had returned.

Fatigue, coupled with pain in my back and wrist, engulfed me, making my eyelids heavy. The rhythmic purr of the engine and the gentle sway of the vehicle had me struggling to keep my eyes open, but then I glanced out the window, and it finally sank in where we were.

We had made it back to the mansion.

An iridescent sheen rolled over the lawn, faintly lighting up the dark night. It enhanced the Victorian sensibility of the stone edifice that towered in front of us. Dark green slanted dormers jutted above each window of the top floor, dim golden light peeking through thin white curtains.

A matching stone driveway circled in front of a square porch, and stairs led up to an arched entryway. A dark stone statue of Queen Ambrosia towered in the center of the circle, its long, flowing hair wisping out behind it.

The other two vehicles pulled up behind us. Some of my sleepiness ebbed, and I braced myself for the other guys' stress and anxiety.

When Raven turned off the vehicle, the three of them were already opening the back door near Ryker's head.

Kendric's dark eyes scanned his alpha. Deep lines of worry were etched into his forehead. Xander and Gage flanked him, their bodies coiled with tension despite the exhaustion evident in the slump of their shoulders.

"How is he?" Kendric clenched his jaw and looked at me, not Raven.

I jerked my head back and cleared my throat. "He's stable. His healing kicked in once we removed the knife. The wound has clotted and begun closing, but he's still weak from blood loss."

Gage's shaggy, dirty-blond hair fell over his sparkling blue eyes. "We felt him getting stronger via our pack bond, which is why we didn't try to get hold of Raven while we drove."

"We need to get him inside and in bed so he can rest properly." Briar bit her bottom lip. "That will help him heal."

Nodding, Xander rasped, "Yes." His normally tan skin had blanched, and his eyes somehow seemed more pronounced. "Two of us will need to carry him. Kendric, why don't you get the top half, and I'll carry the bottom?"

Gage stiffened, but then he sagged. He'd been close to death too. "What about me?"

"You need to rest nearly as much as Ryker does." Raven climbed out of the vehicle and shut the door then faced the men. "I don't know everything that happened, but that can be discussed later, since it's clear you're injured as well. You don't want to drop him and hurt him worse, do you?"

Frowning, Gage crossed his arms. "No, but I'm staying right beside them in case something happens and they need help."

Kendric and Xander carefully maneuvered Ryker out of the SUV, supporting his weight between them. Gage hovered nearby, ready to assist as promised. Despite their obvious exhaustion, they moved with practiced efficiency, bodies in sync as they lifted their alpha.

Ryker's head lolled against Kendric's shoulder, his face

ashen in the moonlight. His shirt, torn and stained with blood, clung to his muscular frame. The sight of him looking so vulnerable sent a pang through my chest. He was usually strong and resilient. Everything about this felt wrong, and acid burned my throat.

"And you two need to get clean and rest too," Raven said, nodding toward me. She had to mean the spot between my upper shoulder blades where the enemy had clawed me.

"A shower would be amazing." Briar glanced down at her outfit. "I haven't had a way to clean myself for way too long."

My mouth dried, and my chest burned with anger over her being treated that way, but I'd caused enough problems tonight, so I kept my lips pressed firmly together.

The two of us followed Raven up the mansion's grand stone steps. The ornate wooden doors swung open silently, as if by an unseen force. The foyer's crystal chandelier cast a warm glow over the marble floors and richly paneled walls.

Our footsteps echoed in the cavernous space as we headed toward the living room and kitchen. Normally, the mansion wasn't this quiet due to all the vampires that lived here, but right now we could have heard a mouse fart.

When we entered the living room, the usually immaculate space looked as if a whirlwind had torn through it. Plush velvet throw pillows were strewn across the floor, and an antique mahogany table lay on its side, one leg splintered. Shards of crystal from a smashed vase glittered on the Persian rug like fallen stars.

Half-empty glasses of what looked like blood dotted various surfaces, evidence of the vampires' hasty departure to assist us. The TV hanging on the wall flickered, though it was muted.

As we walked past the kitchen, a little bit of normalcy kicked in. The spotless stainless steel appliances glistened, and the island had been left bare, most likely because the kitchen was rarely used by the blood-drinking vampires.

The guys didn't hesitate, taking Ryker into the bedroom at the end of the house.

Raven turned to Briar and me, her violet eyes sympathetic. "You two need to get cleaned up and rest. Ember, why don't you use the bathroom you've been using? I'll show Briar to one of the other guest rooms with an en suite." She placed a gentle hand on Briar's shoulder and continued. "Come with me, dear. Let's get you settled."

Biting her bottom lip, Briar wore an expression of trepidation.

*It's fine,* I linked. *You even claimed to trust her in the SUV. You know that if I didn't think you were safe, I wouldn't allow you to leave my sight.*

Relief flooded our connection as Briar replied, *You're right. Thank you.*

Raven took a few steps and turned back to look at Briar.

"Sorry, I'm a little out of it. A shower is just what I need." Briar followed her back through the living room.

Wanting to get out of my shredded clothes and wash the blood off me, I headed toward the familiar bathroom, my feet dragging. The gold filigree mirror reflected my haggard appearance—tangled copper hair, dark circles under my eyes, and smears of dried blood across my skin. I peeled off my ruined clothes, wincing as the fabric pulled at the gouges on my back.

The shower's marble tiles were cool under my feet as I stepped inside. I turned the ornate brass knobs, and hot water cascaded all over my body.

The water stung my wounds at first, and I hissed

through clenched teeth. But as the initial shock faded, warmth began to seep into my aching muscles, easing some of the tension I'd been carrying.

I tilted my face up into the spray, letting the water run over my closed eyelids and down my cheeks. It washed away not just the dirt and blood but some of the fear and anxiety of the past few days.

The water was pink from all the blood that had coated me, and the urge to get clean took over.

I grabbed a bottle of shampoo, opened it, and inhaled deeply. The scent of lavender and vanilla filled my nostrils, replacing the stench of copper. I breathed it in and scrubbed my scalp, needing to erase the sticky feeling.

Then I worked in the conditioner and soaped up my entire body. After a lot of exertion, I managed to eradicate every trace of blood, and my wounds ached but in a way that didn't seem disgusting anymore.

If I hadn't been about to fall asleep on my feet, I would've stayed in the shower longer, but that would have to wait for another day.

But when I reached to turn off the water, a loud snarl from outside the bathroom shook the walls. My heart clenched, and my spine tingled in warning.

# CHAPTER SEVEN

Another snarl reverberated through the walls, followed by a crash like shattering glass. My heart raced as I grabbed a plush crimson towel from the nearby rack.

"Where is she?" Ryker's voice boomed, deep and guttural. "Has she left?"

Adrenaline surged through me, chasing away the exhaustion that had settled in my bones. I wasn't sure if he was talking about Raven, Briar, or me, but it didn't matter. He needed to get his ass back in bed so he could heal.

I hurriedly dried off, wincing as the towel brushed over the wounds on my back. Water dripped from my coppery hair, leaving trails down my skin as I snagged the black pajama pants and gray shirt Raven had left for me while Gage replied, "She's in the shower. Chill, man."

As I slipped on the clothes, my back throbbed with each movement. The soft fabric of the shirt clung to my damp skin, and I bit back a hiss as it touched the wounds. Every muscle in my body ached, a stark reminder of the night's events.

"What do you mean she's in the *shower*?" Ryker barked,

his voice closer now. "She said she'd leave as soon as she got Briar back. She needs to go!"

The intensity in his tone sent a shiver down my spine, even as my heart ached at how desperate he sounded for me to be gone.

Kendric said tightly, "Ryker, you need to rest. You've lost a lot of blood. Ember is safe, I promise you."

I yanked open the bathroom door, straightening my shoulders, ready to confront Ryker and figure out what the hell was going on. But once I stepped into the hallway, I froze at the sight before me.

Ryker stood in the middle of the corridor, his massive body taking up most of the space. His bare chest heaved with each ragged breath, and he winced with every movement, likely in pain from his injury. The muscles in his arms and back were coiled tight, and the bandage wrapped around his torso was already stained with fresh blood, a harsh reminder of how recently he'd been at death's door.

His wild eyes locked onto mine, the gold flecks in them practically glowing in the dim light, the iridescent sheen still missing. His expression smoothed out, softening the hard lines of his face. But just as quickly, that relief morphed into something darker, more primal.

"You," he snarled, taking a step toward me. "You need to leave."

His words knocked the breath out of me. After everything we'd been through, after he'd nearly died saving my sister, this was how he wanted things to end? My chest constricted painfully, and a lump formed in my throat.

"Ryker, I don't underst-stand." My voice, barely above a whisper, cracked. My wolf whined and growled. She was hurt just as much as my human side but also didn't like how vulnerable I sounded. I hated how much his rejection hurt, how it echoed Reid's public humiliation.

He moved closer, his towering frame dwarfing mine. The heat radiating off his body enveloped me, a glaring contrast to the chill that had settled in my bones. His scent —a heady mix of pine, rain, and something uniquely Ryker —enveloped me, making my head spin.

He reached out and gently grasped my shoulder. Pain shot through me, along with the sparks that sometimes came with his touch. But the agony was so strong that I whimpered, unable to hold back the sound.

Ryker dropped his hand and froze. "What the fuck is wrong?" His eyes narrowed as he examined my shoulder.

The sudden shift in his demeanor caught me off guard. One moment, he was demanding I leave; the next, he seemed worried. My head spun, unable to keep up with the rapid changes.

I paused, trying to find the right words so I wouldn't smell like another big fat lie. After breathing the scent of blood for as long as I had, I wasn't convinced I could stomach the stench of rotten eggs. "I'll be fine. Just some battle wounds that aren't nearly as bad as yours." I nodded to his ribs and gritted my teeth so I didn't wince in discomfort. The injuries were scabbing over, getting tighter and more uncomfortable.

Ryker's eyes narrowed as if he could see through my facade. Without warning, he walked around me, his chest brushing mine. A spark jolted between us, but he moved behind me before the moan I swallowed could escape.

His fingers gently brushed my hair aside, exposing the wounds on my back. The light touch sent sparks racing across my skin, a contrast to the dull ache of my injuries. As

Ryker's breath ghosted across the nape of my neck, a shiver rolled through me.

Kendric stood with his back against the wall, his clothes wrinkled and frumpy. Xander slumped across from him with his head hanging low while Gage stood centered behind them with his arms crossed.

"When did this happen?" Ryker's heartbeat remained steady despite the dark tone.

The warmth of his body was intoxicating. Heat emanated from him, seeping into my own skin. My wolf stirred restlessly within me, yearning to lean back into his solid frame. However, I refused to do *anything* like that since he'd made it clear he didn't want me here.

"During a tea party," I quipped, trying to defuse the situation.

He gritted his teeth, the faint sound of grinding enamel making it evident he didn't find me amusing. "Not funny, lil rebel. I need an answer, or I may lose my mind."

I stepped toward the other three to gain a little distance from Ryker and clear my head then used the wall to steady myself.

"I was slashed by one of the attackers when I was trying to protect Gage." I wanted to focus on why Ryker was desperate for me to leave.

He blinked and then scowled. His brows furrowed into harsh lines across his forehead. His eyes darkened, and he hung his head. "I can't believe I forgot that happened."

I lifted my hand to touch his arm, but my shoulders and back screamed in protest, and my mind yelled *no*. He'd made it clear he wanted me gone.

Instead, I forced a small smile. "You were severely injured and losing blood like crazy. I don't even know how you held up that long, so I'm not surprised that the end of the fight is fuzzy for you."

He ran a hand through his already disheveled dark hair, his slightly trembling fingers betraying his exhaustion and the toll his injuries had taken. "That's still no fucking excuse. Did you get hurt anywhere else that I should remember? Or after I passed out?"

His gaze raked over me. The intensity of his stare made it hard to breathe, and I reacted as if he could see right through me. I fidgeted under his scrutiny, hyperaware of every ache and pain in my body.

"Other than my hand, there's nothing too extreme." I raised my right hand to show him the claw marks on my wrist. "Just some scrapes and bruises. Nothing that won't heal."

Ryker frowned, and he looked to his three packmates. The intensity in his gaze made me glad I wasn't on the receiving end of it.

"How much trouble did she cause?" He arched a brow.

The three men exchanged uneasy glances, but Kendric cleared his throat and met Ryker's eyes. "She fought well and didn't cause any panic."

Xander nodded, his stoic expression softening slightly. "She was instrumental in our escape this time. Without her, we might not have made it out."

Ryker tilted his head. "What do you mean?"

The tension in the hallway thickened as Kendric opened his mouth to respond.

Before he could get a word out, Gage lifted both hands. "We should discuss this later." He shot a warning glance at the others. "You need to rest, Ryker. We can fill you in on all the details once you've recovered more."

Ryker tilted his head back and clenched his jaw as he

looked between his packmates. "No, I want to know now. What aren't you telling me?"

The air crackled with unbroken tension. Xander straightened from his spot on the wall while Kendric kept his expression carefully neutral.

Gage stood his ground, dropping his hands and facing his alpha head-on despite not being well. "All right, if you insist on knowing now..." He tilted his head to the side as if steeling himself. "After you were stabbed and lost consciousness, we were still surrounded. Ember... She ordered us to leave her behind so we could get you, Gage, and Briar to safety."

Ryker's eyes glowed and widened as his wolf inched forward.

I fought the urge to back away from him. I didn't want him to think I was intimidated. I wasn't—I just didn't like seeing that anger directed at all of us.

A low growl rumbled in his chest. "She did *what*?" His hands clenched at his sides.

I bristled, anger flaring in my chest. The accusation in his voice stung even though it wasn't directed at me. How dare he talk about me as if I wasn't standing right here? As if my choices and actions didn't matter? If he wanted to act like I wasn't part of the equation, I would force him to reconsider.

His nostrils flared. "You listened to her? She's not your fucking alpha—and you left her behind, injured like this?"

"Hey!" I snapped and stepped forward despite the protest of my aching muscles. "I'm right here. Don't talk about me like I'm not in the room. If you've got a beef with anyone, it should be *me*. "

The corners of his lips tipped upward before the skin

around his eyes tightened. "Did you just say *beef*? How old are you? Eighty?"

"What?" A salty taste filled my mouth. "Are you really insulting me right now?"

"Oh, if I wanted to insult you, I would've chosen something a lot worse than that." He grimaced. "I should have known you'd do something reckless like this. It's a pattern with you, isn't it? Always putting yourself in danger, always trying to be the hero."

His words stung, but I refused to back down. I lifted my chin, meeting his fierce gaze head-on. "I wasn't being a *hero*. I did what I had to do to protect everyone. You were unconscious and bleeding out. Gage was struggling to stand on all four legs. Briar needed to get to safety. And Kendric and Xander had to work together to carry you. Also, I was the only one who could see the attackers. What else was I supposed to do?"

He lifted his right hand to his mouth and bit his finger before pointing at me. "You are supposed to stay with the group, to let us protect you."

"I don't need your protection, and we never agreed to you all protecting me. You only promised to help me find Briar, remember?"

Instead of answering my question, he bared his teeth at the others. "Why the hell did you listen to her?" he growled, the tone low and dangerous. "She's not your alpha. I am."

The hallway seemed to shrink as Ryker's anger filled the space.

Kendric stepped forward, his broad shoulders tense. "Ryker, you were unconscious and bleeding out. We had no better option. Ember's plan was the only way to ensure everyone's survival. If we'd stayed, we would have been more vulnerable."

Xander lifted both hands placatingly. "You have to understand. We were surrounded, outnumbered. Ember's quick thinking saved us all."

Groaning, Gage closed his eyes and shook his head just as Ryker's almost exploded.

"Enough!" he roared. His face had flushed an angry red, the veins in his neck standing out prominently. His nostrils flared as he took sharp, ragged breaths. "You all were outnumbered? And you *left* her? What the fuck is wrong with you three?"

My jaw dropped, and my blood heated. "Are you seriously blaming them for following my orders? *I* made the call, not them. They wanted to stay and fight, but I knew it was hopeless. I ordered them to leave so that at least most of us would survive."

Ryker's mouth twisted, and his eyes narrowed into tiny slits. His entire face contorted with visible rage, and I took an instinctive step back.

"And that makes it okay? You were willing to sacrifice yourself? To throw your life away?" he spat.

"I wasn't 'throwing my life away,'" I snapped, my voice rising. "I was trying to save everyone else's. Including yours, you ungrateful ass!"

"Ungrateful? Me?" Ryker pointed at himself. "I took a knife for your sister because she's important to you. How the hell am *I* ungrateful?"

My heart clenched. He was right. He'd risked his life protecting my sister.

But then his hypocrisy dawned on me, reigniting my anger. "That's exactly my point." I placed my hands on my hips, ignoring the way my muscles screeched in protest. "How is what I did any different? I stayed behind so the three injured people and the two carrying you could get back safely. I made the same choice you did—to protect the lives of others at the risk of my own."

He shook his head vehemently, his dark hair falling across his forehead. He winced again, his hand instinctively going to his injured side. "That may be, but it doesn't change the fact that what you did was reckless and foolish."

"Then I guess we're both idiots." I wasn't going to let him get away with the double standard.

"No, we're not. You're leaving, and I'm going to stay and get proof of what the Blackwoods did to our families and take them down." The iridescent sheen glistened over his eyes for a few seconds, hiding his irises, but it faded as quickly as it had appeared. "Your life means more to me than mine."

"See, you're desperate for me to leave. Why act like you care when you don't?" I hated how my heart panged so badly it felt like it could implode.

Ryker's body went rigid. The fierce anger that had contorted his features moments ago melted away, replaced by an intensity that made my breath catch.

"Do you really want to know why?" he rasped.

The sudden shift in his demeanor caught me off guard. I swallowed, my heart pounding against my ribs. Part of me wanted to say no, to run away from whatever revelation was coming. But a larger part of me needed to know. I needed to hear him say he hated me.

"Yes," I whispered, the word barely audible even to my own ears.

Ryker placed a finger under my chin, forcing our gazes to connect. He opened his mouth, and I tried to prepare myself for the agony sure to come.

# CHAPTER EIGHT

H e closed his eyes and took a deep breath, his finger still tilting my chin up. When he opened them again, the intensity in his gaze made my breath catch. The gold flecks in his eyes seemed to dance in the dim light of the hallway, drawing me in.

"The last thing I would ever want," Ryker growled and winced, "is for you to leave."

My heart skipped a beat, and that damn foolish hope bloomed in my chest despite my best efforts to squash it.

The other three guys began moving away, but I couldn't tear my gaze from Ryker's.

His thumb caressed my jawline, making me tremble. "Every fiber of my being wants you to stay. To keep you close, to protect you, to..." He trailed off, swallowing hard before continuing. "But being here puts you in constant danger, and I'm willing to let you walk away because it might be the only thing that can save your life."

My mind reeled as I tried to process his words. The sincerity in his voice and the vulnerability etched across his features were so unexpected that the ground shifted beneath my feet.

The hallway seemed to fade, leaving Ryker and me in our own little bubble. His hand dropped from my chin, but the phantom warmth of his touch lingered. I searched his face, looking for any sign of deception, but found the golden flecks in his eyes pulsing with what could only be described as raw honesty.

My heart raced, and an imprudent part of me wanted to lean into him, to let him chase away the trauma of the night. But another part—the part that still bore the scars of Reid's rejection—screamed at me to run.

Running wasn't an option. Briar wanted to stay, and Raven had made me realize that, even though I had good intentions, it wasn't the right choice. Still, that didn't mean I wanted to fall for another man. Even if my wolf and my body wanted to be around him.

I took a shaky breath, trying to center myself. The air crackled with unspoken emotions. Emotions I couldn't address, or they would lead us into unknown territory and might ruin whatever Ryker and I had now.

Yet, Ryker's scent enveloped me—pine, rain, and something uniquely him. My head spun and my wolf stirred restlessly.

"I..." My voice cracked, and I cleared my throat. "I appreciate your concern. But I'm not leaving. Not now, not when there's still so much at stake."

His eyes widened for a brief second before he schooled his expression into neutrality. "What do you mean? The whole time we were searching for Briar, you made it clear that you would be leaving to protect yourselves. That was the plan, and you need to go tonight."

The urge to step toward him was so hard to fight that I

planted my feet on the hardwood floor. "I know what I said, but things have changed. We're going to remain here and gather proof of who is behind all of this so we can end the slaughter of innocent supernaturals."

Ryker's jaw clenched, and the muscles in his neck tightened. "Trust me. I will handle this. If you go, I'll even give you daily updates. You and your sister need to leave now. I need you to be safe so I can focus and not constantly worry about you."

Butterflies took flight in my stomach, so to overcompensate, I gave my voice a hard edge. "You can't even see the enemy. I *can*. That gives us a small advantage, but only if I stay. If I leave, then Briar and I won't be here to help protect our friends, and I refuse to be like our so-called allies after Reid rejected me."

He clenched his hands. "Ember, you don't seem to understand the danger you'd be putting yourself in. These enemies are unlike anything we've ever faced before. Look at what happened tonight. I don't even understand how we got away."

"I think Raven and the other vampire guards scared them off with the additional manpower." My mind raced back to the chaotic escape. "The shadows were everywhere. We couldn't even rely on our sense of smell to track them because, even when they were right on us, their scent was faint. They chased us when we tried getting to our vehicles."

I closed my eyes as the vivid memories flooded back. The air had been thick with the acrid smell of fear and blood, punctuated by snarls and screams. Iridescent shadows had darted between the trees, their bodies not clearly detectable except for their head and when they stretched out their arms.

"But then there was this...shift. Like a ripple in the air. The shadows hesitated, some of them even recoiling. The strange feeling I had that night at the park when Simon got away returned, and they couldn't reach me. There was... like...a barrier between us."

Ryker scowled. "The witch who cloaks them must have alerted them that the vampires were there to stop them."

I nodded, the pieces clicking into place. "That makes sense. It would explain the sudden retreat. But it also means they're more organized than we thought. More dangerous."

A chill raced down my spine as I considered the implications. These weren't random attacks but rather a coordinated effort by a group with access to powerful magic. The realization made the night's events even more terrifying.

"Exactly," Ryker growled, his eyes flashing. "Which is why you need to leave. *Now*." But even as he said it, I could see the conflict in his eyes.

My heart sputtered. I despised how much I loved seeing that he didn't want me to go. No matter how hard I tried to pull back from him, my heart and wolf still urged me closer. If I didn't know any better, I would think he was my fated mate...but that was impossible. Reid was the one Fate had chosen for me. The twat.

His jaw clenched and unclenched and the muscles in his neck strained again as he fought some internal battle. Despite us not touching, the buzz that so often hummed between us faintly covered my body, drawing me to him despite my best efforts to resist.

When I hesitated to respond, he smirked as if he'd gotten through to me.

*Nope.* I refused to allow him to believe I'd submitted to his request. He wasn't *my* alpha. "I've already told you. I'm not leaving. Not now when there's so much at stake."

"Dammit, Ember." He lifted his fisted hands, and his ab muscles constricted. A new line of crimson appeared on the bandage over his wound. "You don't understand what you're getting yourself into. This isn't just about you anymore. It's about the safety of everyone around you."

I lifted my chin. "And that's exactly why I need to stay. How can I turn my back on you, the guys, Raven, and Queen Ambrosia after everything you've done for me?" I raised my hands, trying to ignore the way my injury screamed in protest. "And, again, I am the only one who can see these shadows! That alone is reason enough for me to stay and help. "

He hung his head, his broad shoulders slumping. The fight seemed to drain out of him, the fatigue and pain of the day catching up. "You don't understand," he breathed. "When you're in danger, I...I lose my mind. It's like everything else fades away, and all I can focus on is keeping you and everyone you care about safe. Tonight, when I saw that knife coming for your sister, I didn't even think. I just moved. Because I knew losing her would destroy you, and I couldn't bear to see you in that kind of pain."

A lump formed in my throat. Whatever restraint he'd had before tonight had vanished. He'd lowered his guard and exposed his true feelings.

I realized something just as disturbing, and my knees weakened.

*I'd do the same for him. I would risk my life for him and anyone he truly cares about.*

Whatever we felt for each other was dangerous, and I had to fight it and keep a level head for both our sakes. "I would've never wanted or asked for you to risk your life to protect her. Losing you would be just as painful as losing her." The last sentence tumbled from my mouth without permission, causing my stomach to churn.

His head jerked back ever so slightly, and a faint grin spread across his face. "Is that so?"

My heart raced, and my wolf stirred. She wanted to embrace him, to bridge the gap between us and offer comfort.

But that was the worst thing the two of us could do. Allowing a relationship like this to become stronger would only cause more problems for us later on.

I had no choice but to hold firm, even if it was the last thing I wanted. My tongue felt heavy as I forced out the words. "Yes, it's true. Losing you would be devastating. But that's exactly why we need to stop *this*." I pointed at him and then back to myself. "Whatever is happening between us, we can't let it continue."

A flicker of hurt flashed across his face and he stilled.

"We have to focus on the bigger picture," I continued, forcing the words out even as every fiber of my being screamed in protest. "There's an enemy out there butchering packs, using magic we don't understand, who probably has a witch that might always be with them. We can't let our emotions make things even more complicated, no matter how much we want to."

His expression softened, and he took a step closer to me, increasing the buzz in the air between us. The heat radiating from his body enveloped me, and his scent filled my nose.

"Ember," he said huskily, "I've been trying to fight this since the moment I first saw you at the ceremony where you were to become Reid's. The reason I was so desperate to leave you after I pulled you from the river was because you tugged at my humanity when I didn't want the distraction, but thankfully, Kendric, Gage, and Xander showed up and forced my hand. Every day, this connection between us strengthens, and when I woke up in the car after you removed the knife from my side, it intensified tenfold. I can't keep denying what's happening between us."

His fingers ghosted along my cheek. The familiar tingle sent shivers down my spine.

He continued, "Every time we're together, the fire ignites hotter. My wolf paces in agitation, yearning to be closer to you. The connection between us... It's unlike anything I've ever experienced."

The words resonated deep within me, waking something primal and undeniable. The air between us seemed to crackle with electricity.

I swayed toward him, drawn by an invisible force bolstered by his admission. My resolve weakened with each passing second, and my wolf howled in frustration as I kept standing in place.

I longed to trace the strong line of his jaw and run my fingers through his dark hair.

Every cell in my body surged to life, wanting me to cave.

But I wouldn't.

Especially since whatever was brewing between us seemed even stronger than my connection to my fated mate, Reid. It shouldn't be possible. Yet I couldn't deny the truth.

Cold tendrils of fear circled my heart. It raced, pounding so hard I was sure Ryker could hear it. My wolf shifted within me, clawing at my insides, desperate to take control.

*No*, I shouted at her, renewing my determination. Reid's rejection had destroyed my entire world. If I gave

Ryker even more of my heart and soul, how would I survive when he changed his mind?

I averted my gaze to the wood floor and ran my toes over the cold smoothness, trying to focus on anything but the man standing before me, baring his soul. I traced a particularly prominent knot with my big toe, feeling the slight indentation in the otherwise flawless surface.

The chill of the floor seeped into my skin, a stark contrast to the warmth radiating from Ryker's body. I could feel his gaze on me, intense and unwavering, but I couldn't bring myself to meet his eyes. Instead, I fixated on the thin gap between two planks, imagining I could slip through it and disappear into the foundations of the house, away from this moment and the impossible choice before me.

I winced. "I'm sorry, I can't." A knot twisted in my stomach as I waited for his fury and the kind of brash retort I learned to expect from the man I'd first met.

But that wasn't what I got.

Instead, silence filled the hallway. The tension was so thick a bitter metallic taste sat heavy on my tongue. The spark between us continued to sizzle, which meant he was still there, so I forced myself to lift my head, bracing for anger or disgust.

What I saw damn near shattered my resolve.

Pain had etched deep lines around his eyes and mouth. The golden flecks in his irises had dimmed, and his broad shoulders slumped.

He looked defeated. A disconcerting contrast to the powerful, commanding alpha I'd come to know.

"I understand," he said softly, his voice barely above a whisper. "And that's why I'll wait until you're ready. Until I've proven to you that I want you and will always remain by your side." He let out a shaky breath. "Because I know why you're saying no. I've been doing the same thing when it comes to you, but I learned tonight that if something ever happens to you, it will kill me. So why waste time?"

The raw honesty in his voice made my heart clench painfully. I searched his face, looking for any sign of deception, and waited for the smell of a lie.

I found neither.

The hallway seemed to shrink as he closed the distance between us.

I should've stepped back, but when his hands cupped my face, I couldn't move. The strength of our connection kept me anchored in place.

He licked his full lips, bringing my attention to them.

"I will prove myself to you, lil rebel, but until then, can I kiss you once to get me by?" he murmured.

# CHAPTER NINE

Every rational thought in my mind screamed that this was a mistake. That I should push him away, maintain my distance, and protect my heart from even more future pain. But I stood frozen as his thumb traced the curve of my jawline, sending electricity racing through my veins. Close like this, I could see the tiny scar through his left eyebrow, the one that somehow made him look even more dangerously attractive and served as a reminder of all the battles he'd fought and the pain he'd endured.

"Ember," he whispered, his breath warm against my lips. "I need an answer."

The air between us felt charged with electricity. That was bad enough, but my heart sensed more at the same time —the possibility of us together, which caused my wolf to howl with something visceral and undeniable. She stirred deep within me, her excitement a tangible pulse that seemed to synchronize with Ryker's own energy.

This was it. The moment I told him no...but no words came. Instead, my traitorous body forced my head to nod.

He smirked, closing the distance between our faces.

I grew dizzy and couldn't stop the pinpricks that ran through my body. One kiss wouldn't change anything between us. We'd already shared several at the alpha meeting for show.

But when his lips touched mine, everything else in the world disappeared. His kiss was soft yet demanding. A perfect balance of gentleness and raw passion that had heat spreading throughout my body. His warmth enveloped me, chasing away any lingering worries, and he slid his hand from my jaw to the back of my neck, his fingers threading through my damp hair, tilting my head.

My wolf surged forward, her excitement a wild, primal energy that threatened to consume me. She wanted this—wanted *him*—with an intensity that scared me. The connection between us wasn't just physical; it was something deeper, more profound than should be possible.

The kiss was nothing like the ones we'd had earlier. Those had been strategic, calculated performances designed to maintain a facade. This was a raw, unfiltered connection that bypassed all my defenses.

His lips moved against mine, and his minty taste had my heart stuttering. Each subtle movement sent waves of electricity dancing through my entire body, making every nerve ending sing in awareness.

When he tugged at the hair that his hand had fisted to tilt my head, he deepened the kiss, and I moaned softly.

He growled and pressed our bodies together. The sound was possessive yet tender, a contradiction that mirrored everything about our complicated connection.

Sparks of ecstasy thrummed between us, and something tugged at my mind. There was something I needed to do, but I couldn't remember what it was. All I could focus on was his taste, smell, and the feel of his body pressed against mine. But our clothes still served as a barrier.

Needing to eliminate the problem, I slid my hand down his chest, enjoying the curves of his muscles and the way he trembled under my touch. Affecting him made me feel even more brazen and out of control.

My fingertips reached the top of his abs and continued to lower to the waist of his black sweatpants when the movement sent pain flaring through the injury to my upper back.

I jerked back and gasped as reality crashed around me, and suddenly, I remembered what I had meant to do.

Stop the kiss.

Instead, I'd lost my damn mind, and if I hadn't been injured, Fate knows how far I would've gone.

Ryker's brows arched, and he loosened his grasp and detangled his fingers from my hair. "What's wrong? Did I hurt you?" His low tone echoed with worry.

I shook my head, both answering him and trying to dispel the haze from the kiss and the intoxicating pull of his presence. "No. It wasn't you...it was me," I stammered, my heart racing from how close I'd come to losing myself. "I put too much strain on my injury."

"Oh, well..." His cheeks reddened. "If you want to go to our room, I have no problem removing your shirt and my sweatpants so it doesn't hurt you again," he breathed.

My wolf inched forward, wanting me to rub my body all over him so we'd smell like one another. But I bit my bottom lip and averted my eyes, trying to keep myself grounded and not lose control again.

Of course, my gaze trailed down him, and my body heated even more...until it landed on the white dressing of his wound. Fresh crimson blood seeped through the formerly pink-tinged bandages that served as yet another reminder of why we couldn't let ourselves get carried away. As much as every fiber of my being wanted to continue what we'd started, the reality of our situation was critical for so many reasons that we couldn't even count them on both hands.

"We need to get you back to bed," I said firmly, forcing my voice to remain steady.

He let out a hasty breath. "I'm so glad to hear you say that. I'm *all* about continuing what we started."

"That's not what I meant." I pointed to his torso. "You're bleeding again. We need to check your wound."

Ryker's confident smile faltered, replaced by a grimace of pain. The flush that had colored his cheeks moments ago drained away, leaving him pale and drawn. His hand instinctively went to his side.

"It's nothing," he tried to protest, but the weakness in his voice betrayed him.

I stepped closer, my hand reaching out to steady him. The moment my fingers brushed his skin, the spark flared between us, stealing my breath.

I took a step back. The connection ebbed but didn't completely disappear. My wolf whined in protest, desperately wanting to be close to him, but I refused to tempt Fate again.

I'd already messed up by kissing him; if I didn't set boundaries now, there was no telling what I might do next. "No, you need actual rest. Right now. You nearly *died* tonight and lost a shit ton of blood."

His jaw clenched, but the pallor of his skin and the faint beads of sweat on his brow proved he was worse off than he was trying to appear. His usual alpha confidence wavered, replaced by a vulnerability that made me want to protect him.

"But I didn't." He winked. "And kissing you and feeling your body against mine is my preference over sleep."

I crossed my arms, arching an eyebrow. "You're bleeding again, and you just spent the last hour arguing with me and then kissing me instead of letting your body heal. I c-can't see you like that again." My voice broke on the last sentence, which I hadn't even meant to say. I didn't need to encourage him.

The corners of his mouth tipped upward, and he leaned in closer. "You can't see me like what?"

I swallowed hard, schooling my expression into one of neutrality even as the heat of embarrassment flooded my body. "Injured. Bleeding out. Vulnerable."

"Ah..." The flecks of his eyes warmed to gold. "So you do care. I'm glad we can both admit that now because I'd die to protect you and everyone you love."

When the hallway remained clear of the scent of sulfur, I couldn't even question whether he meant those words. And the scariest part was that I felt exactly the same way about him. In less than two weeks, he'd become just as important to me as my sister, which shouldn't have been possible. I wasn't certain how we'd evolved from him being a gruff asshole to begrudging allies to *this*. I'd fallen for him.

But I couldn't admit that to him.

"I care about a lot of people's survival," I deflected, crossing my arms. "Not just yours."

He chuckled, a deep rumbling sound that unnerved me. "Nice try, lil rebel. But we both know that's not entirely true."

The way my heart skipped a beat told me we needed to end this conversation before things got even more complicated between us.

His eyes sparkled. "So, are you still going to sleep with me?"

Memories of sharing a bed for the past several nights sprang into my head. Every inch of me wanted to, which meant I definitely shouldn't. "No, I need to check on Briar and stay close to her. But I'll walk you back to your room to make sure you actually rest."

He pouted. "Afraid you won't be able to control yourself if you get too close?"

I rolled my eyes, refusing to take the bait. "More like afraid you'll reopen that wound and bleed out in the middle of the night."

"If it weren't for your sister..." He shrugged and then grimaced from the movement. "I'll allow you to have this one night." He stuck out his tongue and wrinkled his nose, but his irises darkened in discomfort.

I couldn't prevent the small smirk that played across my lips, which helped hide my worry. "Oh, you'll *allow* me? How *gracious* of you."

His eyes narrowed, and he growled, "Watch it, lil rebel. If you keep it up, I may have to punish you."

I placed my hand on his lower back, and the inexplicable connection surged again. My hand trembled, and my wolf whimpered and howled in frustration. She wanted to connect with him physically, but she also wanted him not to die. Fortunately, him not dying won, so I managed to guide him forward with a level head.

I noticed a slight tremor in his legs and the way his breath caught with each movement. He must have been so eager to find me that adrenaline overrode his pain. But after we'd kissed, it had caught up with him again.

As we reached the kitchen, I noticed Raven's and Briar's scents, but this time, they were stronger, like they'd recently been here. As we continued to the door that led to the soundproof bedroom with the four queen beds, the scent went the same way.

When I opened the door, each Grimstone pack member was on his bed, and Raven and Briar were standing in the center of the room.

All eyes turned to us, and Raven's attention went straight to Ryker's wound. I tried to gauge her reaction, but her expression didn't change.

"How," she enunciated with deadly calm, "did his wound manage to reopen?"

Kendric, Xander, and Gage tilted their heads expectantly, not even attempting to come to our defense, while Briar's hand pressed against her chest. Her wet hair appeared auburn and clung to her violet top, leaving wet spots.

"I'm still waiting for an answer as to why the three of them let him leave this room." Briar glared at the three pack members who had left Ryker and me alone in the hallway.

On the left side of the room, Gage lifted both hands from his bed. "We did go after him, but he wouldn't listen. He had to see if Ember was still here, and when he found her, the two of them argued. The three of us were super uncomfortable around the sexual tension brewing between them, and we felt like perverts watching. The entire hallway smelled like a brothel, so we left. We knew Ember would take care of him, or he would link to us if needed."

Ryker snarled, and his body coiled, making it wet with fresh blood. "Never. Compare. What we share. To. A. Brothel."

Briar's head tilted back, her gaze darting between Ryker and me. The room fell silent, the only sounds the rapid beating of my heart and Ryker's ragged breathing.

If I could have cloaked like our enemies, I would have done it in that moment. Ryker wasn't even pretending to dislike me anymore, which meant I had to do something before people got the wrong idea.

I cleared my throat. "This conversation is irrelevant. Ryker and I weren't having sex, so comparing us to a brothel is extreme. My priority is getting this pain in the ass in bed so he can heal."

Ryker's head jerked in my direction as he snorted. "*I'm* the pain in the ass? Maybe you should go look in a mirror."

I forced my jaw to drop, trying to relieve the tension in the room. "What? Me? *Never!*" Maybe I made things challenging for people who didn't agree with me, but I only did what I felt was right.

"Hey, tonight you were a badass." Xander bowed his head. "If it weren't for you, I'm pretty certain none of us would've made it out alive."

"Then I can count on you doing me a solid." I directed Ryker past the others and nudged him down on the bed. The descending moon shone through the windows, giving the room a twilit feel. "Keep his ornery butt in bed until he sleeps for at least twelve hours."

A loud groan escaped Ryker as he lay down. His blanched skin was almost *vampire*-light. My gut twisted. I wished I could take his pain away.

"They won't have to." Ryker shifted in bed, the skin around his eyes tight. "I'll do it for you."

From his spot across from Ryker's bed, Kendric chuckled. "Of course he will."

My spine stiffened, and my injury throbbed. Awareness that everyone was still watching us seized me. Still, I couldn't stop myself from pushing his hair out of his eyes. "Please get some rest. Okay?"

His eyelids were already drooping. "Anything for you."

A lump formed in my throat, and my vision blurred. I needed him to turn back into the guarded asshole who wasn't so kind to me. I needed some distance. And fast.

I took a few steps back, already missing the heat of his skin. I forced myself to turn my back on him and focus on Raven. "Where do Briar and I sleep tonight?"

"We brought an air mattress in here. I figured the six of you would want to stay together." Raven gestured to a mattress placed against another wall, already blown up, with covers and two pillows.

My shoulders relaxed. I hadn't realized that I'd been nervous about not being in the same room as the Grimstones. "Thank you."

"You're welcome." Raven yawned and opened the door. "All of you, rest. The vampires are on their way back, so once I debrief with them and the queen, I'll be getting some sleep myself."

The guys didn't hesitate, relaxing in their beds as Briar and I headed to our mattress. The two of us got settled, with me taking the side where I could check on Ryker easily. I whimpered faintly as I tried to get comfortable.

Briar linked, *What exactly happened between you two in the hallway?*

*Nothing that's*— I stopped myself because what I was about to say was a lie, and she'd know. *Worth talking about.*

*Oh, come on.* I felt her flip toward me. *I need to know. We tell each other everything.*

However, now that I was clean and lying down, my muscles ached and my eyelids grew heavy. I focused on listening to the sounds of Ryker's breathing. *Can we talk about it tomorrow? I'm exhausted.*

She sighed dramatically. *Okay, fine. But you're not getting out of it tomorrow.*

Fate knew she'd make sure I didn't.

I closed my eyes, missing the warmth of Ryker's body near mine.

---

Something cold brushed my cheek, and my eyelids fluttered. The coolness felt like being cast in shadow. The faint scent of something familiar hit my nose.

*No.* This couldn't be happening.

# CHAPTER TEN

**M**y pulse thundered in my ears, and my eyes popped open as I sat bolt upright. Sunlight streamed through the massive windows, casting long golden rays across the floor. Each of the Grimstone pack members slept deeply, their chests rising and falling, and Briar lay beside me, completely unaware, her light copper hair splayed across the beige pillow.

There was nothing out of place or amiss.

Everything inside me screamed that someone had been in here. I leaned toward the edge of the bed where the person must have stood in order to touch me, and for a split second, I smelled the faint aroma again before it vanished into thin air.

It didn't smell like shifter but rather like the unique floral odor I'd smelled in the woods when Ryker had been hunting Simon.

The scent didn't seem to come from this world.

My wolf stirred, her magic pulsing through my body as if in agreement.

My mouth dried and my head spun.

Had I really just thought a scent couldn't be from this world? Maybe I was losing my mind after all. I wanted to focus on locating the enemy and eliminating the threat, but if my grief kept messing with me like this... I needed to take the time to mourn my parents, the loss of my alpha and pack.

The mere thought of them had pain radiating from my heart to the missing spots of my packmates. My lungs struggled to breathe, and I slowly lowered myself back on the bed, not wanting to disturb anyone.

My wolf, however, disagreed. She prowled inside me, her senses heightened and alert.

I agreed that something seemed off, but I wasn't sure if I could trust my logic. The cold touch, the ethereal scent—it felt like a warning, a whisper from something beyond my understanding.

Of course, my traitorous gaze landed on Ryker. He lay on his back, his chest rising and falling steadily. Even in sleep, he looked powerful, his muscular frame proof of all the training and fights he'd had all his life. Seeing the return of his olive complexion soothed some of the ache in my heart.

Despite it being late morning, I knew all of us needed more rest, including me. I turned on my side so I could see anyone who stood beside me. Every time I tried to close my eyes, they popped back open, scanning the area for the intruder.

I concentrated on my breathing, attempting to calm myself, but my mind wouldn't stop, and my wolf hadn't settled.

That cold touch replayed across my cheek, worsening my unease.

My wolf paced restlessly inside me, her senses alert.

The magical energy that always hummed beneath my skin felt different—sharper, more electric. The air itself seemed charged with an otherworldly tension that made the hair on the back of my neck stand on end from both some unexplained recognition and fear.

The weight of the unknown pressed on me like a palpable force that made it hard to breathe. I had to get a grip. I couldn't allow fear to dictate my actions, especially when there was no way someone could have been in the room without one of us stirring... and yet, I couldn't shake what I sensed was true.

I took a deep breath, focusing on the familiar scents of the room—the comforting musk of Briar, the earthy aroma that clung to Ryker, and the faint traces of the other pack members. But the memory of the phantom scent lingered, a ghostly reminder of the presence that had invaded my space.

*Stop. No one could've been here.* I was allowing my imagination to run wild *again*.

I fidgeted, trying not to wake Briar, my wolf growling softly in my mind, urging me to take action.

I glanced at Ryker, his face serene in sleep. I walked toward him, needing to close the distance between us. With each step closer I took, the panic that clawed inside me eased. I propped myself against the wall near him, and eventually my wolf relaxed, and my heart returned to its normal rhythm.

The late-morning light filtered through the windows, casting golden rays across Ryker's sleeping form. My fingers itched to trace the line of his jaw to confirm he was still alive and healing, which was asinine. I could hear his heartbeat and see his chest rising and falling.

I kept my hands firmly at my sides and played the

events of the past night through my mind—the attack, the knife, Ryker's willingness to sacrifice himself for Briar —for me.

The connection between us seemed to buzz through the distance like a tangible vibration. It felt even more intense than it had last night, as if a bond continued to strengthen between us. Yet, I had already found my fated mate, and he'd rejected me and killed my pack. Nothing should be able to form between Ryker and me, and yet, each day, spending time away from him became harder and harder.

None of this made sense. Fated-mate bonds were predetermined before either person was born because their soul was split in two.

I leaned against the wall and slid to the wooden floor. As soon as my butt hit the ground, Ryker stirred.

He moaned softly and moved closer to the edge of the bed near me.

I closed my eyes as if that would somehow make him unable to see me if he leaned over, and I wondered if the crackle I sensed in the air had become some sort of beacon to him. Hopefully, the sensation was one-sided.

His eyelids flickered open. For a moment, he scanned the room before his eyes finally locked on me, and somehow, the friction between us sizzled with even more energy.

"Are you okay?" he rasped. His brows furrowed, and he lifted his head then winced, one hand covering his injury. "What's wrong?" He studied my face and tried to sit up.

"I'm fine." I lifted both hands. "You need to stay still and not aggravate your stab wound," I deflected, hoping that he wouldn't ask me what was wrong again.

He lifted a brow, studying me with an intensity that made me want to squirm. If I'd believed a person could see into someone else's soul, I'd swear that was what he was doing to me, and it was unnerving.

"You're pale," he said, his voice rough from sleep. "Paler than before you went to sleep. And you look..." He paused as if searching for the right word. "Unsettled."

I swallowed hard, aware that my attempt to appear calm had failed spectacularly. "I'm fine," I repeated, the words hollow even to my own ears. Still, that was the one thing I could say that was true—right here next to him, everything seemed fine... Right. The cold touch and floral smell damn near disappeared from my mind.

"I know this trick. You say you're fine to skirt around the problem." He placed a hand on the side of the bed and sat upright. "Let me see your back. You could be bleeding again."

Damn him for being smart. I'd thought that, with his wounds, he would be less aware of mine.

I sighed, knowing he wouldn't relent. "My wound has been healing. It doesn't hurt as much since I woke up."

"Then there's no risk in humoring me, is there?" He placed his hands on the white sheets, readying to throw them off.

"Fine. Stay put. You're still hurt." I got up and sat on the bed with my back to him. Our proximity turned the air into static electricity but without the shocking discomfort. I pulled my hair to the side so he could see my upper back. Before I could reach back to pull the collar lower for him, calloused fingertips touched the skin at the back of my neck and did it for me.

Electric pulses shot throughout my body, and my breath hitched.

His fingers traced the edges of the wound, sending

shivers down my spine. Each touch was featherlight, and the heat of his breath hit my skin.

My wolf and body wanted to tremble, but I clenched my teeth, refusing to show how much I wanted him.

"That's amazing." A low rumble vibrated from his chest. "Your wound is almost completely healed. How bad was it?"

I bit my lip, fighting the urge to lean into his touch. "It was super raw, and it hurt to move. It's now just a tad uncomfortable, and I was surprised how much it had healed by the time I woke up." Despite my best efforts to remain aloof, my body betrayed me, leaning ever so slightly into his touch.

"Well, if your wound didn't wake you, what did?" His hands stilled on my back, setting the one section he continued to touch ablaze.

I hesitated. The memory of that cold touch and the lingering floral scent felt too surreal to explain. I'd sounded paranoid in front of him too many times. My imagination must be playing games with me.

"Just a bad dream." I didn't know what to say to him other than that. It was the truth.

He exhaled and dropped his hand, and I immediately missed his touch. He said, "It was an awful night. I'm not surprised. Why don't you tell me about it?"

I tensed. The last thing I wanted was to speak out loud that my mind was continuing to play tricks on me. "I'd rather not. It's over, and..." I stopped myself, realizing that I'd almost said that being next to him made things better. It did, but I didn't need to voice that. "It was just a dream."

But as the words left my mouth, a warning shot down my spine—a sensation so sharp and sudden it made me stiffen. It felt exactly the same as when we'd been in the woods with Simon.

I turned to look out the windows that faced the woods. There had to be someone watching us.

A breeze picked up, swaying the blades of grass. The sunlight still filtered softly through the window, casting golden patterns across the wooden floor. The other pack members continued sleeping deeply, their chests rising and falling steadily.

Yet, the feeling persisted.

My wolf whined softly in agreement. But I couldn't pinpoint exactly what and where the sensation was coming from. Nothing seemed amiss inside or out.

"Hey, I get it. Not seeing the face of the enemy is scary. Come here." He scooted over and lifted the edge of the covers. "Lie down and get some more rest."

Everything inside me yelled at me to oblige him. "I can't." I shook my head, and when the corners of his lips angled downward, I realized that I might have hurt his feelings. I continued, "If Briar wakes up and I'm not on the air mattress, she'll freak out."

He smiled, and my mouth watered. With his still-sleepy eyes and morning scruff, his entire essence made him delicious. He reached out and gently touched my arm. The connection between us responded immediately, sending a warm tingle up my skin. "I won't sleep. If she starts moving, I'll wake you first," he promised. "Trust me."

"I *do* trust you." When I hadn't, it was a lot easier to fight this connection between us. "It's just more important for you to get rest, especially since my wound has healed almost completely."

He licked his lips, and jealousy churned in my stomach. I wanted it to be my tongue, not his. The spicy scent of arousal wafted around us, calling my ass out. My face heated, and I wanted to cover it with my hands, but that would only make things worse.

His eyes glowed faintly, his wolf no doubt catching the scent.

I opened my mouth to argue, but the vulnerable look in his eyes stopped me. His injury was still fresh, and despite his bravado, he needed rest more than I did.

"Before you answer, just know that, after seeing you like this, there's no way in hell I'm falling back asleep anytime soon. The best way for you to get me to rest again is to lie down here with me until we're both calmer, and then I swear I won't harass you when you leave to crawl back in bed with your sister." He pouted a little, though his eyes danced with mischief.

I hadn't seen this playful side of him before, and it melted my heart a little. Before I could stop myself, I exhaled. "Fine, but only for a few minutes."

Ryker smiled, and he lifted the blanket higher, creating a warm invitation.

I turned and placed my legs on the mattress but didn't lie down. "We're keeping our hands to ourselves. Got it?"

"Scout's honor." He held up a hand with all fingers straight.

A faint giggle escaped before I could stop it. "It's a three-finger salute, and we both know you were never a scout." I moved to put my feet back on the floor, seeing as he clearly wasn't willing to make that promise. My wolf growled in my head, but I had to ignore her.

"Stop." He nodded toward the bed. "I promise to keep my hands to myself even if I don't want to. Okay?"

"Okay." My wolf huffed as I placed my legs back on the bed and scooted down. He settled the covers over me, and I was surrounded by the best smell in the entire world. Though our bodies didn't touch, I could feel the heat gather between us, and before I even realized it, my eyes were closing.

---

The door to the bedroom banged open, startling me from sleep. I bolted upright as Ryker tried getting up beside me. He groaned, his injury still too fresh for him to move easily.

Kendric, Gage, and Xander were already on their feet while Briar gaped from her spot on the mattress as Raven strutted inside and slammed the door.

Her violet eyes were laser-focused, her gaze cutting through the room with an intensity that immediately set my wolf on high alert.

"We have a problem," she announced in a voice as cold as winter frost. The air in the room seemed to drop several degrees.

"It better damn well be a fucking good one with how you just marched into our room," Ryker snarled, finally managing to get to his feet.

The urge to reach out and steady him almost took over, but Raven answered, "It is. We have a visitor."

Briar's copper hair was tousled from sleep, and she pushed it out of her face. "Who?"

Raven's gaze swept across the room and landed on me. "Someone who wants to speak to Ember alone."

# CHAPTER ELEVEN

R yker's body went rigid, his muscles coiling as he prepared to strike. "Who is it?"

My heart thundered, and sweat pooled in my armpits. The way Raven's lips pressed together and she straightened her back had my stomach in knots.

Flipping her long black hair over her shoulder, Raven leveled her gaze at Ryker. "I understand that you're smitten with her, but the specifics are none of your business, seeing as they requested to talk with *her* and not *you*."

I sucked in a hasty breath and almost choked. I'd never seen her have an attitude with any of the shifters before. I hadn't expected it.

Considering the way Ryker strode over to her with his hands clenched, he must have felt the same way. With each step he took closer to Raven, the higher Raven lifted her chin.

"Babe, what's going on here?" Kendric rubbed a hand down his face as he stumbled from his bed. "Why are you acting like this?"

She bared her teeth, revealing that her fangs had elongated. "This has *nothing* to do with the Grimstone pack and everything to do with the Sinclair alpha. I'm not sure how many times I have to say the same thing in varying ways. Normally, when my support role for the queen involves wolves, that means Ryker. But it doesn't this time, and it's not my duty to divulge the details to anyone but Queen Ambrosia and Ember."

Ryker stopped about five feet from her. I could've sworn I saw fur sprouting on his arms, which, given the way his alpha power was radiating off him, made sense. I had to do something because him shifting would exacerbate the problem.

"Babe, we've been through too much to play games. Ember is on our team and an ally. Why can't we know who and why?" Kendric asked as he hurried over and placed a hand on Ryker's shoulder like that would prevent him from lunging.

I had to step in, or things were going to continue to escalate. I licked my parched lips. "If I ask who wants to meet with me, will you answer here?" I chose my words carefully, not wanting to make the situation even worse.

She exhaled slightly, her shoulders relaxing. "If that's what you wish, I can. However, it's your choice if you want to ask in front of everyone or behind closed doors."

"Clearly, she wants you to answer here, or she wouldn't have asked that fucking question," Ryker growled, sounding more animal than man.

Raven glowered at him, her nose wrinkling.

Yeah, things were going to get out of hand. Maybe the Ember of three days ago wouldn't have let Ryker hear what was going on, but the Ember of today didn't want to hide things from him. "Who wants to meet with me and why,

Raven?" I added her name so there was no question that I was speaking directly to her.

Her fangs retracted. "The Shae alpha sent a request to Queen Ambrosia via the returning guards to visit with you here around noon. He requested to speak to only you, in my presence, since he'll be on vampire soil."

I threw a leg off the bed and placed my foot on the cold, smooth wooden floor. Bruce Shae was the last person I'd have predicted would want to speak to me, especially since he'd kidnapped my sister.

A snarl erupted from Ryker's chest. "Like hell she's speaking to that bastard alone."

Raven's elegantly arched eyebrow rose, her expression a perfect mask of diplomacy. "This is the way of war. You should know that, based on your family legacy and your own experience. He'll be here within an hour, so I wanted to provide you ample warning."

I glanced down at my thin shirt and pajama pants. This wouldn't do to meet the man I planned to kill since Reid had failed to do so during their attack. I needed him to feel intimidated. He had a reason for coming here, and I suspected it wasn't good.

"I've placed an outfit for you in the bathroom. When you're ready, come into the meeting room so we can wait for him together." Raven turned and vanished, not looking back at Kendric.

Ryker spun toward me, and I inhaled. "Like hell you're meeting him alone," he snarled, his body trembling with barely contained rage. The muscles in his neck strained, and a thin sheen of sweat covered his olive skin. His wound had reopened slightly, a thin line of crimson seeping through the bandages.

"Here comes the temper tantrum," Gage muttered.

Ryker rounded on him and gritted out, "What did you just say?"

Now that his glare was directed elsewhere, I felt like I could breathe again. I'd seen him angry a handful of times, but this was the first time it made me want to avoid his gaze.

Gage lifted his hands in mock surrender while a sardonic smile played across his lips. "Just making an observation to myself about what's going on. That's all."

"So you're good with Ember handing herself over to that jackass?" Ryker's face flushed, reminding me of a tomato.

Xander hung his head. "Let's not argue among ourselves. We have enough enemies without turning on each other."

"Ember would never be an enemy of ours! To insinuate —" Ryker started.

I cut him off. "None of us are turning on each other." I needed the drama to end so I could focus on the real target —Bruce Shae. "One of our enemies is coming to meet with me, so we need to stop wasting time and focus on strategy." My voice rang a little louder than normal, my wolf lacing my voice with power. Though I wasn't the Grimstones' alpha, that didn't mean they weren't affected by my magic.

Head tilting back, Gage's brows rose. "Damn. She's stronger than I remember."

Xander, Kendric, and Gage all looked at me with creased foreheads.

"She may be strong, but I hate that she's conceding to that prick's demand for a meeting." Ryker's breathing turned uneven, and he placed his left hand on top of his bandage. "I don't want you to go in there alone."

My knees weakened a little. "Raven will be with me. I won't be alone."

"I'm not sure if this makes things better, but while I was held captive, they were never cruel to me." Briar sat in the middle of the mattress, watching the whole exchange go down.

Her words hung in the air, and when the scent of a lie didn't hit, I realized she truly meant what she said. I could feel the weight of her statement, the unspoken questions it raised. Still, it didn't change the fact that they *had* held her captive and chained to a fucking bed.

Ryker growled low in his chest, a sound that vibrated through the room. "Don't," he warned, his voice sharp. "Don't even think about trusting him, Ember."

His using my actual name had a lump forming in my throat, but my blood heated with anger. All my attention landed back on him. "I'm not trusting him, *Ryker*," I said, my voice firm. "I have no doubt his *kindness*"—I placed air quotes around the word—"was an attempt to gain her trust so she might tell him something that would help them locate me. But I still need to know why he's doing this. Why he's asking to speak to me alone, especially after we were attacked on his land."

Briar fidgeted, her movements hesitant. "Maybe...maybe he wants to talk about the attacks and explain what happened. Or about the Blackwood pack. Or maybe he wants to apologize."

I frowned, my mind racing. The Blackwood pack had never been a thorn in our sides before, despite their ambition and cunning ways. Our pack had never viewed them as a threat, but we'd clearly underestimated them and the fact that they were a dangerous enemy. To make matters worse, we'd viewed Bruce Shae as a pack friend. Both packs coming together to take us down didn't make sense though. We just wanted to be left the hell alone, but the death of the shifter royals had changed things for everyone. Maybe this was another change.

Ryker stepped closer to me, dominating the space. "I agree we need to know what he wants, but I don't want you in there with only Raven."

I stood my ground, my heart pounding against my ribs. "I have to. This is about more than just me. It's about the pack, about Briar, about all of us."

Briar's shoulders sagged. "I trust Raven, but it would be nice for Ryker to be with you. I don't want anything to happen to you," she whispered.

I felt a pang in my chest, my resolve wavering. But I couldn't back down. Not now, not when so much was at stake.

Raven's words echoed in my mind. *This is the way of war.* She was right. This was a game of power and strategy, and I had to play my part. We couldn't miss out on whatever Bruce had to say, and having Ryker there could freeze him up.

"I'm sorry." I bit my bottom lip. "I have to do this. But I promise you, I won't go in there unprepared, and if anything goes sideways, I can alert Briar through our pack link. Besides, you already look exhausted, so it's better if you stay in bed and get more rest."

A muscle worked in Ryker's jaw, and he scanned me. "Fine." His face tightened. "But I'm not staying in bed. I'll be right outside the door with Briar, so if anything goes wrong..."

Butterflies somersaulted in my stomach, and my chest expanded to the point that it hurt. A small smile tugged at my lips. "I know, and thank you."

The room fell silent, the tension thick and heavy. I

could feel the weight of the coming meeting pressing down on me, the unknown looming like a shadow on the horizon.

I took a deep breath, my wolf stirring anxiously inside me. I could feel her fear, her uncertainty, but also her determination. We were in this together, and we would face whatever came next as one.

Standing in awkward silence wouldn't accomplish anything, especially with the way my skin had started crawling with dread and anticipation while Briar and Ryker studied me with worried expressions.

I'd had enough. "I'm going to change and get ready." I hurried out of the room, eager to process things without being scrutinized. I walked toward the bathroom, hoping that whatever Raven had left for me would make me look strong. I needed to present myself as a force to be reckoned with. I couldn't let Bruce Shae see any weakness, especially since we were in a house full of vampires.

As I stepped into the bathroom, the cool marble beneath my feet made me shudder. The outfit Raven had laid out for me was a stark contrast to my disheveled appearance—black leather pants, a form-fitting top, and a jacket that screamed power.

Thank Fate that Raven had understood the assignment. I shouldn't have doubted her; she'd proven time and time again that she was wise and knowledgeable.

I dressed quickly, visualizing each piece of clothing as another facet of armor that protected the vulnerability I felt inside. Once dressed, I worked my hair into a tight braid, the copper strands gleaming in the faint light. The mirror reflected a determined face, but my eyes betrayed the turmoil within. I placed my hands on the sink counter, trying to get my feet back underneath me. I had to give the illusion I was in control and confident in every way—eyes, posture, and even how I walked and spoke.

When my heart finally calmed to a normal rhythm, I knew it was time to go. Raven wanted me to be in the room with her before Bruce arrived, showing a message of unity and that he was clearly the visitor.

When I exited, Ryker was leaning against the wall in jeans and a black shirt. I could see the outline of the bandage around his rib cage, but him being dressed made his intentions clear.

He would make sure Bruce saw him.

His eyes narrowed as he took in my appearance. "You look the part, but that doesn't mean you have to do this alone. We can still do this together."

*Together.* I really liked the sound of that, but I couldn't jeopardize this chance to get information. I cleared my throat. "If he wanted to meet with you alone, would you turn down his request?"

He opened his mouth to answer, but Raven cleared her throat as a gust of wind hit us and her scent surrounded the two of us. She said, "He's pulling into the driveway. We should get set up."

Set up? I wished there were something we could do to set ourselves up, but we were at the mercy of whatever Bruce wanted to dangle in front of us. Luckily, the only leverage he'd had over me—Briar—was back in my possession.

"Okay." I moved to follow her.

Ryker grabbed my arm, turning me back toward him. His eyes glowed, his wolf coming forward, making me swallow hard. "I'm getting your sister, and we'll be right outside the door. I don't care if he looks cross-eyed, farts weird, or sneezes funny. If something seems off, I need to know you'll let your sister know. If something were to happen to you..." He trailed off, his expression twisting into agony.

My heart thundered as if it were trying to break free from my rib cage. The space between us hummed with electricity, and I wanted to take him into my arms and tell him everything would be okay. But I couldn't for many reasons, so I did the only thing I could do. "I promise."

He exhaled, but he retained his grip on my arm.

"Ryker, don't force things to become tense between us." Raven took a few steps closer. "We need to get into the room before he does so he has no time to settle in."

With a grimace, Ryker let my arm go, and I immediately missed his touch. But before I could do anything, Raven looped her arm through mine and tugged me in the direction of the conference room, the same place where we'd met the first night we'd arrived here.

We entered the house's gigantic foyer with its staircase that twisted to the second floor and a massive window showcasing the mountains behind the mansion. A table to the left was decorated with four lamps and a towering Gothic black cross in the middle.

Raven led me through an archway into a massive office with interior walls made of stone. There was a huge television in the center of the wall directly across from the entrance, where Queen Ambrosia had joined us via teleconference that first night, and a colossal dark cherrywood table sitting in the center in front of it. This time the table was vacant, and the room smelled of old roses, not the copper tang of blood.

Not missing a beat, Raven seated us with our backs to the TV. When Bruce entered, he'd see us immediately.

"Do you have any idea what this is about?" This was the first time I'd gotten to ask her this question alone.

"None." Raven's crimson lips pursed. "But we'll figure it out together."

Somehow that didn't sound as nice coming from her as it had from Ryker, but I believed the sentiment.

Footsteps echoed down the hallway, and soon the door opened, Bruce's tall figure filling the frame.

As soon as his sharp green eyes met mine, the hairs on the back of my neck stood on end. All of a sudden, I realized that I'd done something horribly wrong.

# CHAPTER TWELVE

Seeing Bruce without Ryker beside me felt unbearably wrong. However, I understood why a shifter wouldn't be comfortable with Ryker present, given the stories that had circulated about him and his pack. That was the only reason I'd stood my ground about him not being here, but maybe I'd made a mistake.

Still, I had made the decision, and I needed to see it through. I could change my mind at any time and link with Briar.

Bruce stepped into the room, and when the lights hit his face, I could see the pronounced dark circles under his eyes. They were evidence that he'd had a long night after the attack. His shirt was wrinkled, and his jeans were smudged like he'd been working in the dirt. He shook his head, and bits of soil fell from his salt-and-pepper hair.

"Ember," he sighed as he shut the door. "I'm relieved you agreed to meet with me, especially without the Grimstones."

"To be honest, I'm not sure it was the right call to

exclude Ryker, especially after you held my sister *captive*." My voice trembled with rage, but I took a deep breath, trying to keep my demeanor calm. Losing it wouldn't accomplish anything. I needed to pay attention to every detail, to notice whether he began playing with his words to prevent me from knowing he was lying.

He hung his head. "Despite what you think, I was holding your sister for her and our safety. These times have made trust hard, so I understand your position." His gaze briefly shifted to Raven, who sat calmly beside me, a silent, steady presence. "And when the vampires came to protect us because of you, I realized you leaned toward trusting the vampire queen's right-hand woman, perhaps because you've had to be cautious. Shifters did kill your pack, after all."

I clenched my fists beneath the table. "I find it hard to believe that you held my sister against her will for her and your safety, especially since she knew I was alive."

Bruce settled in the spot directly across from me. He folded his hands on the table and rubbed his eyes. "That's why I'm here—to clear the air and to be transparent with both you and the vampires."

*What's going on?* Briar linked. *Ryker is about to burst through the door.*

A part of me wanted him to, but I feared that Bruce might stop talking if he did, and I was about to get at least an explanation. *Tell him not yet, please. I do plan to ask him to join us soon, but I need time to get one answer.* At that moment, I realized that I *had* to bring Ryker in. We'd agreed to be allies, and he'd proven himself to me. If I didn't invite him in, my words wouldn't match my actions. I'd be pissed too, if the situation was reversed.

"We'd *love* to hear what you have to say." Raven tilted

her head and smiled, though the warmth didn't reach her eyes.

He dropped his hands into his lap. "I had *nothing* to do with any of the attacks. I know suspicion runs deep because you were attacked on my land and I had restrained your sister, but I swear I'm just as much a victim as you." He paused, and the room filled with awkward silence.

A sour taste coated my mouth. "If you don't elaborate on that, then there's no reason for me to stay." I wouldn't be appeased by general statements that could have been constructed to hide the truth and make me believe what I thought I'd heard because the scent of a lie never appeared.

He rolled his shoulders back. "Your pack was slaughtered the very next night after Reid publicly rejected and shamed you."

I snorted so hard the back of my throat ached. "You don't have to remind me. I'm *very* well aware."

"I'm sure you are, but this is part of my explanation." He arched a brow and shook his head. "This is why young'uns don't make the best leaders. They're impatient and run their mouths."

"In this instance, I must disagree with you." Raven leaned back and crossed her legs. "I understand why Ember feels you're evading the question. And I promise, *Bruce...*" She emphasized his first name to be clear that she wasn't showing him proper respect. "I'm much older than you, so I believe my opinion carries more weight."

He leaned his head back and glared at the white ceiling. "I've been mated for over thirty years; there's no winning with one woman, let alone two." He huffed and looked me in the eyes. "Even though I hated the way Reid rejected you, the Blackwoods have always been honest and forthright...or so I thought at the time. When he said something was wrong with you, it altered my view of your pack."

My vision blurred, and my eyes burned as tears filled them. I blinked, holding them back. I wouldn't cry in front of Raven, and I damn well refused to cry in front of Bruce. I wouldn't allow anyone to know that Reid's words had hurt me so extensively.

"So when the Blackwoods alerted us that your pack had been attacked, at first, I was relieved that someone had taken care of a potential problem." He grimaced. "But when I got on-site and saw the way your pack was massacred... It was brutal. Something beyond hate, and I instantly felt awful for being grateful for those few minutes."

Wow. He wasn't holding back. There still was no scent of a lie, which informed me that he was being sincere and brutally honest. "Well, it's nice to know that one of the alphas my father considered a friend didn't celebrate his death for too long."

"You wanted full transparency, so that's what I'm giving you." Bruce crossed his arms, which made him appear more tired than flustered or ornery. "I'm still ashamed that I felt relief, but at that moment, I wasn't picturing your father... I didn't imagine his face, or even yours, as one of the dead. When I saw who had been slaughtered, it truly sank in. And I will never forgive myself for those few weak moments."

*Sis, Ryker is about to lose his shit.* Briar's concern poured from her.

*I need a few more minutes. He's telling me why he kept you captive, and after that, I want Ryker to join us.*

"That night, I tossed and turned, so ashamed that I'd let a friend down. That I hadn't taken his side when his pack and his daughter were being humiliated. Maybe if I had stood beside you, the Blackwoods would've thought twice about attacking your home." He rubbed a hand on his arm. "So I got up and went for a run. And that's when I found Briar washed up on the embankment and barely breathing. In that second, I realized that even though I couldn't undo what I'd done, I could at least try to make a bit of amends for abandoning you all."

I wanted to lash out at him, but I'd made similar mistakes that had gotten me into that situation in the first place. Had I not fully trusted the Blackwoods, maybe I would've seen warning signs.

"And you held her against her will? That's how you wanted to make amends?" Raven chuckled darkly.

"That wasn't the intent." He lifted both hands in surrender. "At first, we restrained her because we feared she might wake up when no one was near and run off. At that point, we hadn't begun to suspect the Blackwoods, but we also didn't know who we could trust anymore. I alpha-willed my entire pack to keep silent about her being with us."

So he had a somewhat reasonable justification for doing it at first. "And why was she still handcuffed when we found her?"

"She was unconscious and recovering for almost a week. We'd begun getting worried about how long it was taking her to wake, but we suspected part of it was the loss of all her pack links. She'd only been awake a few days before you arrived, and when she regained consciousness, she was desperate to get away and wouldn't listen to any reason. She refused to eat, drink, or anything unless she was freed to locate her sister. We couldn't risk her escaping because it would not only bring danger to her but to our pack as well if she told people we'd restrained her."

My heart twisted. I hadn't considered that Briar might have been frightened upon waking. She was more sensitive and warmer than me, and I hated that the thought hadn't even crossed my mind, but now that he said it, it made sense. "She said I was alive, but you seemed surprised to see me at the alpha meeting."

"Because I was." He patted his chest. "I thought she was struggling with grief and her connection to you was one that she had to pretend to maintain. And then, not only did you walk in, but you entered with *him*. The very man who ran from an enemy to protect his own ass."

Hot fury blazed through my veins as Bruce's words hung between us, a challenge thinly veiled as a statement.

"If you speak of Ryker like that again, I'll leave this room and never meet with you again." I had to set boundaries and expectations so I was justified when I attacked him.

Raven adjusted the skirt of her black dress. "You won't need to, Ember. I'll have him removed from the premises because the vampires are allied with both your pack and the Grimstone pack."

Nostrils flaring, Bruce pursed his lips as if he'd tasted something bad. "If anyone is part of these attacks—"

"He's *not*. I can assure you." My voice was steady but sharp as a blade. "He was on the brink of death after taking a knife in the side that had been intended for Briar. If anyone has earned my loyalty and trust, it's *him*. And the vampires showed up tonight because of their relationship with Ryker, not me."

I linked to Briar, *It's time.*

*Thank Fate. Ryker is literally pulling his hair right now.*

Not even a second later, the door swung open, and Ryker entered.

Bruce looked over his shoulder and scowled. "I thought we were going to speak alone."

"I gave you all the time I was willing to without Ryker by my side." I held Bruce's gaze. "From this point forward, Ryker and I are a package deal, with you and anyone else."

Ryker's eyes met mine, a flicker of something unspoken passing between us. He was a force of nature, his alpha energy commanding attention. He marched toward me and stopped once he stood on the opposite side of Raven.

"The only reason I didn't demand to be in here at the beginning was due to my respect and trust in Ember." Ryker wrinkled his nose as if looking at Bruce nauseated him. "The fact that you worked with the Blackwoods to attack us on your land was disgusting."

Bruce's expression became a mixture of anger and anguish, and he slammed his fist on the polished wood of the table. The sound echoed through the room, followed by his booming voice. "You think I'd willingly hand over half my pack to die to collaborate with the Blackwoods? What sort of alpha do you think I am?"

Not missing a beat, Ryker spat, "Apparently the same sort of leader you believe *I* am since you have no issue believing I left my pack, the royals, and my family to die."

"Bruce, we understand your pain." Raven's expression softened as she leaned forward. "But if you can't believe us, why should we believe you?"

"Because I've always tried to do what was right, and now that the enemy has attacked my pack, I want justice for them," he snapped. "When I smelled the spilled blood of those I swore to protect and knew I'd failed them, I vowed to seek revenge, no matter the cost."

After a shaky breath, Bruce stood. "I didn't come here to play games or spin lies. I came because I want answers. If that means I have to align with Ryker, I will because I trust Ember."

I still didn't smell any sort of horrible rotten-egg stench. He had to be telling the truth. If he were cloaked, his scent would be greatly muted, but that wasn't the case.

To end the awkward silence, I cleared my throat. "Did your pack or the vampires find any evidence?" I glanced from Bruce to Raven.

Raven shook her head. "Nothing. The guards updated me, and the only thing left behind was a faint scent of shifter that couldn't be distinguished."

"The exact same situation for all the other massacres, along with being unable to see the attackers... Well, for everyone but Ember." Ryker's jaw clenched. "I don't understand how it's possible."

"Wait." Bruce's head jerked back. "Ember can see them?"

A lump formed in my throat. I didn't understand why I could see them when no one else could. "Well, not *them* but a shadow-like outline."

"That's still better than being completely blind." Bruce pursed his lips. "It has to be some sort of magical spell."

"And we all know a witch lives on Blackwood pack territory," I added, mentally pulling up the image of the witch who was supposed to conduct Reid's and my mating ceremony.

Bruce rocked back in his seat. "True, but she doesn't have the magical capabilities to perform magic like this."

"How do you know that?" Raven steepled her hands together.

"Because the Blackwood alphas have always bragged about their little witch, and one night, they had a little too much wolfsbane and confided to some of us what her specialty is."

My lungs stopped working. "Which is?"

He opened his mouth to respond, but then his eyes widened in surprise.

# CHAPTER THIRTEEN

The room hung in a tense silence, the weight of his unspoken words hanging between us. He shook his head in disbelief and, for a moment, it felt as though time itself had paused.

"Emotion," he muttered, the word tumbling from his lips like a confession. "She can manipulate emotions."

A shiver ran down my spine, and the mating ceremony where Reid rejected me flashed through my mind. The pain, the humiliation, the overwhelming sense of betrayal— it all clicked into place. My stomach churned. "She was the witch overseeing the ceremony where Reid rejected me."

Ryker tensed beside me and growled while Raven tilted her head.

Pressing his lips together, Bruce sighed. "The Black-woods... They've always been protective of her. And after the night that your pack—" He cut himself off and grimaced. "I mean... A couple of days after *that* night, Perry Blackwood was plastered at the bar with loose lips, and he let something slip that someone overheard and asked him to elaborate on."

"She could make me feel something I didn't?" The whisper was bitter on my tongue. I thought back to the rejection, to the way my heart had shattered into a million pieces.

"That was my first thought as well." Bruce lifted both hands. "But he *swore* they never asked her to do anything like that and that fated-mate bonds were completely separate."

Ryker's snarl reverberated off the walls, deep and dangerous. His eyes narrowed. "You're telling me that the Blackwoods had a witch capable of manipulating emotions all this time, and you're just now mentioning it?"

Bruce's jaw clenched, and his hands curled into fists. "I learned of it recently and kept it to myself. Even though Perry didn't smell of a lie, I still didn't know who was trustworthy! I didn't want to expose my knowledge and place a target on me and my pack."

"Which is exactly what happened anyway." Ryker snorted and wrinkled his nose. "Not that I believe that you weren't working with the Blackwoods. Fuck, you could still be."

"I'm not now nor was I ever working with the Blackwoods," Bruce shot back, his voice rising. "And just because they have a witch on-site doesn't mean they can attack like *this*."

My stomach dropped, and my lungs stopped working. "Wait." I swallowed audibly.

Raven leaned forward as if ready to spring into action.

Similarly, Ryker stiffened and scanned the room as if he were searching for the shadow attackers only I could see.

"I've been experiencing creepy sensations like I'm being watched." I trembled, remembering that night in the park and when the shadows were nearly on me but couldn't break through some invisible barrier. "That could be the witch's doing." I paused and bit my bottom lip. "But if they knew we were in the park, why didn't they attack us then?"

Shoulders relaxing marginally, Ryker moved closer to my side and said, "They could have been watching us to see what we were up to. Every time there's been an attack, it's been on a larger pack with witnesses."

That made sense, and if it were true, that would mean that I hadn't been imagining things. Or, I was forced to imagine things, which was a far better reason than me losing my mind.

"Either way, it's time for Bruce to leave." Ryker lifted his chin. "We can't trust him."

Face flushing, Bruce bared his teeth. "If I were lying, you'd know by the smell."

Raven stood tall, looking down her nose at him. "Not if you're working with the Blackwoods and they can cover scents."

"Then you wouldn't be able to smell me at all, or I'd be very muted, like those invisible things that attacked and slayed half my pack." Bruce jumped to his feet, the backs of his legs hitting the chair and scooting it back several feet. "I came here in hopes that we could work together, but you're still treating me as if I'm the one who attacked you. As far as I can tell, not only did every one of you survive, but you managed to free Briar as well."

Hot rage ripped through me, but I bit my tongue to hold back the awful words I wanted to say. I didn't see any sheen masking him like I did with the shadows and Ryker's eyes whenever he changed into a colder and harder person.

I took a deep breath, trying to quell the storm of

emotions swirling inside me. "I'm sorry for your loss." I placed a hand on my chest, acknowledging the cold, missing pack links that I suspected would always feel like ice now. "I do believe that a caring alpha wouldn't agree to anything like that, and if it happened, he would want retribution." I hadn't even realized I believed that until I said the words. The uncertainty of whether he was lying had vanished. With the dark circles under his eyes and his pale skin, I saw this was an alpha mourning his losses. "But full trust will take time, especially after you held my sister against her will."

Bruce's jaw tightened as he nodded slowly. "You're right." He sighed and rubbed his hands together. "I understand why *you* are hesitant to trust me, but I do want you to know that I didn't take keeping your sister lightly. She was near death, and I knew people were hunting her. To help her, I had to ensure she was confined and unable to leave. If I'd seen another choice, I would have made it. But desperate times..." He paused, letting the sentence hang.

That was the thing. I did believe him because I didn't see any magical influence on him. However, I wasn't going against the two people who'd truly had my back since the night I lost everything and almost everyone I cared about. I'd hurt Raven and Ryker enough; I refused to be disloyal to them now. "If you were innocent of working with someone, I would've preferred that you at least attempted to explain the situation to Briar instead of keeping her hostage."

His shoulders slumped. "That was my intention, Ember, but we chained her because we didn't want her to get scared and run, and we couldn't always have someone there with her. She woke up when no one was there and freaked out. Between her dealing with the deaths of your pack and not being able to find you, she wouldn't listen to reason. That was our best choice. When you walked into the bar, I realized I was wrong, and I had to do something about it before Ryker slaughtered our entire pack for holding her."

"You son of a *bitch*," Ryker seethed, his body quivering. "We've never *slaughtered* anyone."

"I realized that when the attack happened on our pack. Pack members alerted me to where you guys were during the chaos because, at first, we were worried that you were behind it. And then a few members saw you were, in fact, being attacked and even injured." Bruce ran a hand down his face. "That's why I risked coming here—I believe your story now, despite hearing that you've beaten people up and tortured them. I only wanted to talk to Raven alone because I knew you still wouldn't trust us."

My heart twisted, and my gut hardened. I wanted to tell Bruce he didn't know the full story and ask who he was to judge, but honestly, I'd done the same thing. I still struggled with how Ryker had handled Simon when I thought about that incident, but I'd been able to push it to the side after seeing the sacrifice he was willing to make to save my sister for me—his own life.

"Every person who was tortured deserved it." Ryker's nostrils flared, and his muscles tensed. "I don't have to explain myself to you, and the only people I've ever killed were the scum who would have betrayed us or harmed us at their first opportunity."

I raised my brows, ready to ask questions, but I'd wait until Bruce left.

"The stories don't include that." Bruce frowned.

"The guilty are about making themselves look better,

not the person who called them on their shit." Ryker crossed his arms, his biceps bulging.

If Bruce didn't leave, I had no doubt Ryker would eventually lose it. His strained expression and the sheen beginning to cover his irises told me everything.

"The three of us need to discuss how to proceed, and then together, we'll decide how to move forward with you and your pack." I inhaled deeply, trying to remain calm, though a warning sensation coursed down my spine.

Bruce studied me, and his face softened slightly. "How can we get in touch with one another?"

Right. I hadn't considered that my phone had been lost during the chaos on his pack lands. "Uh..."

Raven leaned forward and held out a sleek black phone to him. "This is for you to contact Ember." She rattled off the number as he took the phone. "It's secure, and we've taken the liberty of ensuring it's warded against any... unwanted listeners. We've had it for a while in case a moment like this happened."

Bruce took the phone, his fingers brushing against hers briefly. He placed it in his pocket. "Thank you," he said softly. "With the chaos and death surrounding our pack, I hadn't even considered that anyone might be listening in on phone conversations."

A lump formed in my throat. I understood that sentiment way too well. If I hadn't needed to search for Briar, I wasn't sure how logical I would've been. Even though I had her back, I now had an enemy who clearly saw us as a target. All those shadows chasing us couldn't be a coincidence.

The heartbreak of losing our pack hung in the back of my mind like a nightmare and was a constant ache in my heart.

"I believe everyone in this room understands exactly what you're going through. Even the vampires have lost lives at the same hands." Raven touched her heart before her hand fluttered to her side.

Eyes darkening, Bruce nodded. "It's something none of us should've had to endure." He turned to leave, his broad shoulders squared despite the weight of the conversation. The sound of his boots echoed through the room, heavy and deliberate.

When the door to the office closed after him, Briar linked, *I'm following him until he exits the front door to make sure he doesn't do anything.* Her disgust shrank the bond, making my stomach churn even more.

I couldn't blame her for disliking him. He'd held her captive, something she might never get over. I'd tried to protect her all my life, and yet I'd failed, leaving her exposed to more trauma.

Pursing her crimson-stained lips, Raven faced Ryker and me. "He's telling the truth," she said quietly, her voice carrying the weight of her centuries of experience. "No magic was sensed on him when he entered, and he's carrying grief and guilt. But there's also something else— something he didn't say."

She'd confirmed one thing I'd already concluded, but I hadn't picked up on the last one. I rocked back on my heels and lifted my brows. "What do you think it is?"

Raven tilted her head, her obsidian hair catching the light in a way that seemed almost otherworldly. "I think he's scared. Not of us but of what's coming. Whatever happened to his pack...it's not over. And he knows it."

A muscle in Ryker's jaw twitched. "I still don't trust him." He crossed his arms. "Just because your spells didn't catch magic on him doesn't mean he has no spells on him."

I grimaced, remembering the conversation Raven and I'd had just days before we located Briar. She'd told me that the vampires could sense a spell on Ryker, but they kept pretending they hadn't noticed it. That had to be why he was doubting their thoroughness. However, Raven had told me that in confidence, so I'd let her handle the explanation.

Still, keeping it from Ryker now left a sour taste filling my mouth.

"I'm very confident in our magic detection." Raven smiled and clasped her hands in front of her chest. "Is there a reason I shouldn't be? Do you know something I don't?"

Before I could stop myself, I flinched. Ryker had unknowingly stepped into a trap.

Ryker jerked his head back slightly, but I noticed the sheen vanished from his eyes as they quickly widened before he schooled his expression into a mask of indifference. "I'm just questioning whether the spells that trace magic should be replenished. Spells can weaken over time, right?"

"Our spells are replenished as needed to keep them at maximum strength, don't worry." Raven smiled a little too sweetly, enjoying the game she and Ryker were playing. "Unless there's something you need to confess?"

"I don't need to confess anything." He lifted his chin in challenge.

I needed to stop this before we broke into a fight among ourselves. "Now that you two settled that, I think the point is that we don't have to trust him. However, we can update him every so often with low-level information and see if he shares anything with us."

A flicker of frustration burned in Ryker's eyes, highlighting the golden flecks. "You think I don't know that? But what if this is a trap? What if he's playing us?"

"I don't think he is, and until you're comfortable too, we'll be strategic with what we share. If you wind up being right, then we'll deal with it. But for now, bickering among ourselves is only wasting energy and time."

"That's something I can agree with. Even if he's not working against us, he's upset, and I fear he won't make tactical decisions for the next bit because he feels guilty for kidnapping Briar and the attack on his pack." Raven shrugged. "We'd be foolish not to have open communication with him in case he does find something valuable we want to research and act upon."

I nodded. "We need more shifter allies, and I think Bruce has something to prove to himself and his pack."

Closing his eyes, Ryker let out a deep breath. "So we're all in agreement to be careful and discuss what we'll share with him before it happens?"

*He's pulling down the driveway now.* Briar's relief flowed into me, helping to drive some of my stress away.

*Good.* I hated that Bruce being here had impacted Briar so much. I hadn't considered how she'd feel when she saw him, and I swallowed, realizing I'd failed her once again. I wanted to say more, but I had to focus on Ryker and Raven. I could discuss Bruce with her in a bit.

"I can agree to that." I rolled my shoulders back.

Raven steepled her fingers. "As do I. We don't need to share everything with him."

"Fine," Ryker rasped. "But if he betrays us, I get to be the one to kill him."

"Okay." I didn't argue. Ryker's word was law, and if Bruce so much as hinted at betraying us, Ryker would act without hesitation. But I couldn't let fear of uncertainty rule us. Not now.

"So what do you propose as our next step?" Raven propped her hip against the table.

There was only one thing that made sense. "I have an idea, but you're not going to like it."

# CHAPTER FOURTEEN

"Then don't tell us." Ryker's voice was low and sharp. "Every time you have that damn expression on your face, you either do or suggest the kind of reckless thing that drives me insane." His words hung in the air, a challenge.

Raven leaned forward, her dark eyes gleaming. "Well then, I *want* to hear it. I want to hear the sort of suggestions that rumple Ryker's fur."

I hesitated, hating that this would probably upset Ryker, but that didn't change what needed to be done to get one step closer to our enemies. "We need to find a witch." I allowed the words to spill out before I could second-guess myself further. "Someone who can help us discover how this magic works and how to dispel it."

Raven's face lit up with a smirk. "A witch. That's a bold suggestion since they tend to protect their kind, but Queen Ambrosia has an understanding with a powerful witch who lives nearby. One that actually warded this phone." She removed a phone from a hidden pocket in her dress and typed out a message.

Ryker's expression darkened, and he turned away and

began pacing the room with a restless energy. "I don't trust witches. They're unpredictable, dangerous. We can't just go around seeking them out like they're some kind of miracle solution."

I suspected the witch Raven was referring to was the same one who'd cast the spell on Ryker, but he wasn't lying. He didn't trust them. Otherwise, he'd reek right now.

Tossing a knowing glance my way, Raven countered, "What choice do we have? We don't fully understand witch magic; they keep the way their magic works secret for a reason. If we want to understand what the Blackwoods' witch is capable of, then we need insider knowledge."

The tension between them was palpable. Ryker's reluctance was clear, but Raven's determination was equally so. She moved closer to him, her presence commanding attention.

"Think of the bigger picture, Ryker." I added my voice to hers. "If we don't act, more lives will be lost. The packs are already on edge, and without answers, they'll turn on each other. If this witch is willing to give us information, it could change the entire game."

Ryker paused with his back to us, his broad shoulders rigid with tension. For a moment, the only sound was his heavy breathing. Then, slowly, he turned. "Why would they tell us anything?"

"A witch might feel betrayed by one of their own working so closely with a wolf-shifter pack, especially if they're eliminating entire packs. One of the widely known rules among all species of the supernatural is that we must respect balance. A witch aiding the Blackwoods is not respecting that paramount rule. Another witch might see it as a betrayal, a violation of their species' ethics."

"Exactly. Desperate times call for desperate measures.

If our neighboring witch is willing to cooperate, even reluctantly, it could be the key we need. But," Raven added, her voice dropping, "we must be prepared for the consequences. If she's willing to help us, she won't do so without reason. And that reason could come with a cost."

Ryker's jaw tightened, his hands curling into fists at his sides. "Still, she might not want to help us," he argued, his voice low and rough. "Why would she risk her own kind's wrath? Some would see it as treachery."

He was right. I hadn't taken that into consideration. "It still doesn't hurt to ask. The worst she can say is no or not come to the door."

"Don't think she'll help out of the goodness of her heart." Raven's tone was steady and firm. "She'll expect an offer of something in return. Protection, perhaps, or information she might find valuable. There are always those who are willing to take risks for the right incentive."

Ryker's head hung low as if the weight of the world rested on him. "And what if she refuses? What if she turns on us, uses her magic against us?"

Raven shrugged. "We've worked with this witch before, and she'll not want to earn Queen Ambrosia's wrath. Worst case, like Ember said, she'll say no and ask us to leave."

He growled, the sound low and menacing, and then took a deep breath. I could tell the suggestion grated on him, and I did believe he felt like this about the witches in general, but I suspected he feared the knowledge of what he'd done would come out. Whatever magic had impacted him, he clearly didn't want anyone to know about it.

"Fine," he bit out, the words sharp and clipped. "We'll go visit your witch."

Even though it was the right call, I tensed. Ryker was upset, and part of me wanted to say never mind because I didn't want him to feel discomfort. But this whole thing was bigger than him, than me, than everyone in the house. The whole supernatural world could be at risk. Who was to say that the killers wouldn't turn on the witches too? I didn't understand their plan since they were targeting multiple species, but it couldn't be good.

"I'll get a car brought around for the three of us to visit Iskaria." Raven glided to the door.

But as soon as her hand touched the doorknob, Ryker snarled, "Ember isn't going. She needs to stay here where it's safe."

A bubble of laughter caught in my throat. "Not happening. I'm going. This was my idea."

"Agreed." Raven nodded. "Be ready in twenty, and we'll head out then. I'm going to call Queen Ambrosia to inform her of our plan." She slipped out the door, which shut with a loud *thump*, leaving Ryker and me alone.

Suddenly, I felt pressure all over my body, as if I were submerged under water. Ryker faced me from the other side of the table, a vein bulging between his eyes.

Clearly, the conversation wasn't over.

"You're *not* going." He took a step closer, his movements deliberate, each muscle in his body coiled and ready to spring. The bandage beneath his shirt was visible through the fabric, a stark reminder of the wound he'd barely survived. Yet, despite his injury, there was no weakness in his stance. He was every inch the alpha, commanding and unyielding.

I held my ground, my heart pounding in my chest. "Ryker, listen to me—"

"No, you listen," he cut in. "You're not going. It's too dangerous. You're not some soldier to be sent into battle.

You're—" He stopped as though the words had caught in his throat.

"Reckless?" I finished, my voice steady despite the turmoil inside. "Or maybe just a liability?" I added, a hint of bitterness creeping into my tone.

His lips pressed into a hard line. "You're not a liability," he rumbled, his voice softening slightly. "But you're also not invincible. Your sister needs you, and you know the risks. Why would you even suggest this?"

My blood boiled. I knew what he was doing by playing the sister card. "It sounds pretty safe, based on Raven's take. And this war needs all hands on deck. Briar made me understand that, and it's why we stayed. I'm going. Besides, it makes more sense for me to go than you. You're still healing. You can barely—"

"I'm *fine*," he snapped. His hand went to his side, where his injury was. The movement was quick, but I caught the flicker of pain that flashed across his face before he masked it. "If that's why you're going, I don't need you putting yourself in danger because of me."

"It's not just because of you." Now that he'd brought his condition to my attention, I realized there was no way in hell he was going anywhere without me. "I can't let fear dictate my choices. I want to avenge my pack just as much as you want revenge for what they did to yours. It's not fair for you to try to hold me back when I want the same thing as you."

He stalked around the table toward me until our faces were only inches apart. "I'm saying we can't afford to lose you," he whispered.

My lungs stopped working. "If we don't work together, then the next time, the shadows might kill one of us, if not both. You can't protect me from everything." My voice was barely above a whisper. "And even if you could, I wouldn't let you. I'm not some fragile thing that needs to be coddled. I'm a shifter, Ryker. I can fight. I can handle myself."

We stared at each other, tension crackling between us like a live wire. Then, without warning, Ryker reached out and brushed my cheek. His touch sent a jolt of electricity through my entire body. I wanted to step closer to him and feel more of what was between us.

"You don't understand." Pain etched lines into his face. "If something happens to you...I wouldn't survive."

I turned my face away and took a step back, needing to clear my mind. "It's still not your decision. I want to tell you to stay put too, because the thought of you in danger kills me. But it's not my place to circumvent your decision, and if I try, all we'll do is argue."

He closed his eyes for a long moment before opening them once again. "You're right, but dammit, I hate the thought of you leaving this place. It's the safest location we've got for now."

Memories of the cold caress and the unfamiliar yet delicious floral scent that I'd detected for seconds flashed through my head. It had happened here, and the Blackwood witch couldn't have been messing with me with her magic. With their safeguards, the vampires would've known. So what had that been? "I'm not sure if we're truly safe here either."

He scowled. "I guess you're right. Fine. I'll link with the pack and let them know where we're headed, and we can go to the car."

I relaxed. The argument between us was over...at least for now.

He reached out again like he wanted to take my hand but stopped himself.

My heart sped up, and I wasn't sure if it was from antic-ipation, disappointment...or maybe both.

He turned and strode out the door. I followed, ignoring the twinge in my heart from him not taking my hand.

It was better if we didn't get more invested in each other.

At the front door, I linked with Briar. *Ryker, Raven, and I are going to visit a witch the vampires are familiar with to see if she can provide any insight into the magic being used by the Blackwoods.*

*Be careful. I can't lose you—for so many reasons.*

Her worry swelled into me, and I replied, *And I feel the same way about you.*

The bright sunlight was a blinding contrast to the dim interior of the mansion. A black Mercedes SUV gleamed in the driveway, engine humming, the vampire queen's statue behind it giving the impression that the queen was watching us.

"Are we all ready?" Raven called from behind the wheel.

Ryker nodded, opening the front passenger door for me before awkwardly climbing into the seat behind me.

I slid into the seat, feeling cool air brush against my skin. The leather seats creaked softly as I settled in. Raven put the car into drive, and soon the mansion dwindled in the rearview mirror.

"How far away is the witch?"

"About five miles," Raven answered, and then we fell into silence.

My mind churned. I didn't know what was to come or if this would get us any answers. I just hoped the witch didn't ask for too much in return.

Raven navigated the winding roads, the only sound the

hum of the engine. The woods around us were dense, the trees casting ominous shadows on the ground, reminding me of the attackers.

I turned my attention to the window, watching the trees blur past. Sunlight filtered through the glass, but even its caress couldn't chase away the chill of the unknown that settled in my bones.

After several minutes, the trees thickened, and Raven's hands tightened on the steering wheel. My pulse quickened. Ryker stayed silent behind me.

"It's right here." Raven nodded at a turn up ahead.

We took the curve, and a clearing with a wooden cottage sitting in the middle appeared. It was small, almost diminutive, but there was nothing quaint about it. The thatched roof was a tangle of moss and overgrown vines, and the walls seemed to lean inward as though the house were listening. Smoke curled lazily from the chimney, carrying the faint scent of burning herbs—something sharp and unfamiliar that made my nose twitch. The windows were small and round, their panes cloudy with age, giving the illusion of empty, staring eyes. To one side grew a garden of herbs, most likely for spells and potions.

Raven pulled up about ten feet from the front door and parked.

"We need to stay close to each other," Ryker muttered and opened his door.

He'd get no argument from me. The three of us got out, and my skin began to crawl. Something felt off, but I wasn't sure what until I noticed the faint iridescent sheen covering the entire area.

"Let me knock first so I can explain to her who we are." Raven headed to the door.

But then I realized another element felt off. I could smell only rosemary despite the garden and the moss.

"Guys, something isn't right." My gaze darted to the woods as Raven reached the oak door with intricate carvings of runes and symbols.

"What do you mean?" Raven's brows furrowed as she knocked. "She's a little quirky, so—"

The door creaked open like it hadn't been fully closed, and Raven froze.

Ryker came up beside me, placing his hand on my arm like he was ready to drag me away at any moment.

"What the hell?" Raven rasped as she opened the door wider...and then she gasped.

# CHAPTER FIFTEEN

The door creaked open, revealing a dimly lit interior that seemed to swallow the light from outside. The air inside was thick with the scent of burnt herbs and something metallic, like blood, but faint. However, the pressure inside was more intense.

A lump formed in my throat as I realized that something had changed in me. I didn't understand how I could feel this magic so strongly, but the new warm pulse inside me that had appeared after my pack had been slaughtered heated even more.

Ryker's grip on my arm tightened, his eyes narrowing as he scanned the room.

The cottage was in disarray. Shelves were overturned, their contents scattered across the floor—jars of strange, glowing liquids, bundles of dried herbs, and books with worn leather covers. As I stepped farther inside, the hum of residual magic lingered, tingling against my skin and making a thicker, iridescent sheen inside. In the center of the room, a large circular symbol was drawn on the floor in what looked like ash and blood. It throbbed faintly, a dark, ominous energy emanating from it.

Spinning around, Ryker studied the area outside for an enemy. Something was wrong, and for some reason, I couldn't ignore the urge to investigate inside.

Removing my arm from his grip, I stepped into the cottage, past Raven, as her fingers moved across her phone. My boots crunched on broken glass and herbs, and the floor groaned. The weight of the magic in the room pressed on me, and shadows twisted in every corner, but none of them formed a remotely human presence.

Raven's movements were cautious as she scanned every inch of the space. "This isn't right," she muttered. "She was always so careful."

I knelt down, my fingers brushing the edge of the symbol. It was icy to the touch, and it seemed to pull at me like it was trying to draw me in as the new presence inside me flared in warning. I jerked my hand back, my breath catching. "This feels...cold—like a void. Whatever she was doing here, it wasn't good."

Ryker raced inside to the far side of the room, his back to the wall, his eyes never leaving mine. "We need to get out of here now. Either something horrible happened to her, or this is a trap."

There was no sign of the witch. No scent, no trace of her presence beyond the lingering magic. It was as if she had vanished into thin air.

I stood, my eyes meeting Raven's. "She's gone," I said, my voice barely above a whisper. "But she didn't leave willingly."

Raven's jaw tightened. "It has to be the Blackwoods."

A tremor ran down my spine. If the witch had been taken and so recently, we were running out of time. "We need to see if we can pick up a trail outside of whatever was spelled here." I turned toward the door. "Now."

Before I could move, Ryker caught my arm, his touch firm. "Like I said, this could be a trap."

"But what if it's not?" I snapped, pulling free. The idea of abandoning someone who might need our help had me wanting to scream *no*. How many more innocent people were we going to lose along the way?

"Ember, listen to me. You can't rush into this. We don't know what we're dealing with. If this is a trap—and it does feel like one—then we need to be smart about it. We can't help anyone if we're dead." Ryker approached me slowly as if I were a wounded animal.

Despite a part of me agreeing with him, my feet remained rooted to the spot. "And if it's not a trap?" I countered, my voice soft but stubborn. "What if she's still alive? What if she needs our help right now and we just...leave?"

"As much as I was hoping for her to help us, she is a morally gray person." Raven continued to scan the area, her brows furrowed. "That's one reason I wanted to come talk to *this* particular witch."

That had to be why the Blackwoods came here. If the witches had a network like wolf shifters did, then their witch would be able to locate any of her species that were close by and determine if they were a threat.

He placed his hands on my shoulders, the electric buzz of his touch sizzling right into my soul. "We can locate other witches. She's not the only one."

He was right, but...dammit. I'd lost almost my entire pack, and now I was letting another person down. "People just keep dying." Maybe I was being weak, but something in my soul called for peace. This pointless killing was far more than heartbreaking.

Raven's phone buzzed, breaking the moment. She glanced at the screen, and her expression hardened. "It's the queen."

Coldness swirled inside me, stealing what little warmth I felt and agitating my wolf. It seemed to focus on my heart. "What's wrong?" If she said the mansion was under attack, I was going to lose my shit.

"She sent over the name of another witch who lives nearby." Raven pocketed the phone and headed for the door. "She's ten miles south of here. Apparently, she owes Queen Ambrosia a favor that the queen can call in."

Ryker dropped his hands and opened the front door. "Then we need to move before the Blackwoods take her as well."

I suspected he finally agreed that we needed a witch to help us. If Iskaria was alive, then she might be begging for death, depending on her situation. "Let's not waste any time."

The three of us darted out of the house, and I wasn't tempted to glance back. The chill began receding from my body, and the closer we got to the car, the more comfortable my wolf became.

Whatever had happened around and inside the cottage didn't feel natural.

When we reached the car, we all jumped in and slammed our doors, the sound echoing through the heavy silence that followed. Raven's hands moved swiftly to the gearshift and then the steering wheel, her eyes fixed on the winding road ahead as she drove. The forest blurred around us, the trees twisting into dark, ominous shapes that seemed to close in with every mile.

Ryker sat behind me, breathing heavily. His fear and

frustration were evident, and I had no doubt he wished he'd fought harder to convince me to stay behind at the mansion.

And that was why we shouldn't go further in any sort of relationship. We couldn't waste time and energy on each other when our entire species was on the line.

Knuckles blanching from her grip on the steering wheel, Raven pressed her lips into a firm line. Her phone buzzed again, and she glanced at it before tucking it back into her pocket. "The queen's contact is named Elara. She's...reluctant to get involved, but she's agreed to meet with us."

"That doesn't sound too promising," Ryker bit out with a hint of a snarl.

"Well, right now, it's the best we have." Raven glanced in the rearview mirror and hissed. "We'll be there in ten minutes, so she won't have much time to change her mind."

But we all knew that ten minutes might already be too late if the Blackwoods had been informed of her.

The road twisted and turned until Raven finally turned onto another narrow dirt path. The car bounced roughly, the tires crunching over gravel and pine needles. The trees here were older, their trunks thicker. I could feel magic before we saw anything. Waves of iridescence and faint wisps of shadows were already shimmering into my vision.

"We must be close," I whispered like I was afraid the witch could hear me.

Raven took another curve, and another wooden cottage came into view suddenly as though it had been hidden on purpose or by magic. It was even smaller than the first one, the roof sagging under the weight of years and the windows cloudy with grime. There was no warmth in the sight. Instead, I again became uneasy, feeling that we were being watched.

We pulled up to the front, and Raven turned off the engine. "Stay sharp." Then she reached for her door.

I jumped out of the car, eager to get to this witch before the Blackwoods arrived. I hurried toward the front door before Ryker got out and could stop me. He growled, a low, rumbling sound, but I didn't care. The Blackwoods could roll up at any moment, and we needed to learn everything we could before they arrived.

Ryker caught up to me, and his hand brushed mine, giving me another jolt. He scanned the perimeter while Raven moved ahead of us, her steps silent, her dark hair blending into the shadows, especially with twilight approaching.

When we made it to the edge of the small front porch, the front door creaked open and a low, commanding voice cut through the chill of the evening air. "Stay where you are."

A woman with a slender frame stood just beyond the threshold, silhouetted by the dim light of a flickering hearth. Her sharp, pale-green eyes gleamed with a mixture of suspicion and wisdom. Elara.

She stood tall with her shoulders back, wisps of iridescence wafting from her and making it clear that her magic was ready to attack and she would not hesitate to defend herself.

My body froze. I hadn't expected a warm greeting, but this was cold and standoffish.

Clearly feeling the same tension, Ryker tried to step in front of me.

Raven stopped and lifted both hands. "We mean no harm. We were sent by Queen Ambrosia. She said you would be willing to help us."

The lines of tension in Elara's face deepened, and her

gaze landed on Ryker. "Queen Ambrosia has been holding this *favor*"— her nose wrinkled in disgust—"over my head for decades, and I was ready to fulfill it and move on, but not when you bring *him* to my door."

Ryker flinched before resuming his normal guarded stance.

My jaw wanted to drop, but I managed to keep it closed. I could only assume she sensed whatever Raven suspected Ryker had let a witch do to him that caused his irises to be covered by that sheen at times.

He stood tall, but I could see his back and neck tighten. He didn't realize it, but he'd just confirmed to me he was hiding something.

"Ryker?" Raven glanced over her shoulder at him. "What's wrong with him?"

I pivoted so that I stood next to him, not wanting to miss any facial expressions he might reveal.

"Nothing is *wrong* with me." Ryker's hands fisted, but his face remained a mask of indifference. "All we're here to do is get some guidance on how to find the people responsible for killing packs and nests and abducting the witch we tried to go to first."

Elara's head jerked as she took a step back into the cottage, where the sheen made it a little more difficult for me to see her despite her pale skin. "A witch is missing? Who?"

"Iskaria," Raven answered quietly. "In the thirty minutes it took for us to talk to her, get ready to leave, and drive there, she vanished into thin air."

"Oh goddess." Elara clutched a hand to her chest. "Why would she be taken?" Her brows furrowed, and her eyes darkened.

"We suspect she knew something that the Blackwoods

don't want us to learn." I wrung my hands, trying to expel my nervous energy. I didn't like the way she was studying us, as if she could see more than I wanted her to.

"Blackwoods?" Elara tilted her head. "I've never heard of that coven, so you should leave." She tried to close the door, but Raven blurred and caught it before she managed to shut it an inch.

Ryker took a few steps forward, and Elara lifted her free hand, readying to perform magic. I grabbed his arm and yanked him back to me, my pulse racing. Ryker getting closer to her had put her on edge.

"The Blackwoods are a shifter pack, not a coven." Raven leaned against the doorframe, making it clear she had no intention of leaving despite the threat of magic.

"We don't get involved in pack business, and frankly, we try to stay out of vampire situations as well." Elara's lips pressed into a thin line. There was a flicker of something in her eyes, a reluctant concern she tried to mask. "The vampire queen may think she can call in favors, but I am not one to be swayed by debts alone."

As the dim light of the setting sun cast long shadows across the cottage, the air grew thick with mistrust. I got a sense that she was done talking with us, and that would be detrimental. We needed something to impact her. "The Blackwoods are slaughtering packs, including mine, and they took out a large vampire nest in the middle of a vibrant town. They have a witch tied to their pack who must be aiding them."

"That's not possible. Witches don't align with other species—it disrupts the balance." Elara shook her head, but she scowled as if she finally believed me.

"The Blackwoods have crossed a line; why would they stop at just killing vampires and wolves now that they've taken Iskaria?" Raven dropped her hand from the door, practically challenging Elara to close it now. "You have a traitor in your ranks."

Elara's expression faltered, concern crossing her face before she masked it again. "Iskaria was a reclusive soul, preferring the solitude of her craft. If she's gone, it's not by choice."

Now that she might believe us, we needed to capitalize on that while she was still listening. "That's exactly why we need your help. The Blackwoods are using the witch affiliated with their pack to hide them from sight." I was going to tell her that I could still see their shadows, but I paused. She didn't need to know that because it was something I couldn't explain. "Also, their scents are repressed to the point that you can't tell where or who each one is. If they can do that, they're a threat, not only to the packs but to your kind as well."

"I can't believe someone would betray their own kind like this," Elara spat. "The witch who is helping them has the ability to cloak. That magic is rare. It's not just about hiding—it's about erasing someone's presence entirely, including her own. Finding someone like that won't be easy."

Raven froze, and Ryker interjected, "Do you know where we might start?"

Elara's lips pressed into a thin line, and she turned away, her movements deliberate. She paced the small space between the door and the room lined with bookshelves holding dusty jars. "I know a name. A witch who *might* still be alive. But I can't promise anything. She's...elusive. Dangerous, even. If she's working with them, she'll be hidden close to the Blackwoods in the forest. That sort of magic requires close proximity."

"Well, their witch lives with their pack." I'd never realized how separate witches kept themselves from most of us because I'd grown up with the knowledge that a witch lived among a pack. "So that makes sense."

"No, this witch would need to live in the woods to harness enough magic to pull that stunt off." She shook her head. "They must have two working with them, both of whom will be close to them."

Finally, a lead. Not an easy one, but a lead nonetheless. "Is there a way to tell if Iskaria is still alive?" I had to ask because Briar was right. We couldn't run from this.

Elara pursed her lips like she'd tasted something bad. "I can't tell you that—only *he* can." She pointed right at Ryker.

# CHAPTER SIXTEEN

M y head snapped in Ryker's direction. Raven's eyes narrowed, but the corners of her lips tipped slightly upward. She was no doubt thrilled that he was finally being called on his shit.

Ryker wasn't amused at all. His nostrils flared, and his breathing quickened. "What are you talking about?" His voice was low, with a hint of menace lurking beneath the surface.

Shaking her head, Elara *tsk*ed. "Don't play dumb. There's no way you aren't aware of the spell that's been placed on you. You had to sacrifice a piece of yourself to gain it. It isn't natural, and it's one for which even witches struggle to understand the impact. It turns you into a different person—so long as the witch is still alive."

He flinched, and my breath caught. His gaze darted to me, then to Raven before he turned back to Elara, his expression strained in a mask of controlled fury.

I wanted to ask what spell, but Ryker was barely keeping it together. I didn't want to add to the already volatile tension, and I seriously doubted he wanted Raven to know all about it.

"I'm still the same person. What are you insinuating?" Ryker crossed his arms, trying to move in front of me again.

I suspected he didn't want me to see his reactions, but tough shit. I edged between him and the wall of the porch so that I could see everyone's face. Nonverbal cues were even more important than words, and not everyone realized that. Sort of like most people didn't realize using sour cream in the batter would make a cake moister and richer.

The air shimmered faintly in front of Elara, indicating that her magic continued to strengthen within her. "I'm not insinuating anything. I'm telling you the truth. The magic within you—whatever it is—ties you to Iskaria. If she's alive, you'll still be affected by the spell that links you two. But if she dies..."

Ryker fisted his hands, his knuckles white. "That doesn't make any sense."

"And that is why you shouldn't mess with things you don't understand." Elara shook her head. "You're connected to her as long as the spell is a part of you, but if she dies, there will be nothing left to sustain the spell."

I watched him, my pulse racing. There was something in his eyes, something he didn't want to admit even to himself. Whatever he had done, Elara must be right. He hadn't thought it through.

Raven looked skyward. "What exactly has he had done to himself?" She turned toward Elara for answers.

A muscle in Ryker's cheek twitched. For the first time ever, I caught a glimpse of defeat in his eyes before the sheen appeared, covering the color once more.

"It's not my place to tell you." Elara crossed her arms, making it clear that we'd overstayed our welcome. "But what I will say is this: You deserve a warning. Whatever bargain you made, whatever spell you've tied yourself to, it's not something to be taken lightly and may result in horrible things happening."

Ryker cleared his throat. "I'm fine."

"Are you?" Raven placed a hand on her hip. "Because ever since you left the mansion alone that one day and came back, you haven't been acting like yourself."

"Yes, I have," Ryker snapped, his voice rising. "Is there anything else you can tell us about the cloaking?"

For a second, I thought he might attack Raven, but thankfully, he reined himself in. Whatever spell was on him, he had desperately tried to hide it and clearly wasn't happy that he'd been outed. Little did he know, Raven and Queen Ambrosia had known about it since the day he'd had the spell cast on him.

Raven messed with her phone, perhaps messaging Queen Ambrosia to inform her that Ryker's secret had finally come out.

Despite my dry mouth, I placed a hand on Ryker's arm for support. However, the electricity that usually sprang up between us was gone. My wolf whimpered loudly in my mind.

For a moment, I didn't think Elara was going to respond. Then she took a shaky breath and dropped her arms. "No, I can't tell you more. Like I said, witches with that power are rare and usually stay isolated. You have a better chance of locating her than I do."

I rolled my eyes. "I'm assuming witches can sense each other's magic and figure out where one would most likely be." We weren't stupid, and she had to realize that.

"Even if I had more to tell you, I wouldn't." Elara's eyes darkened. "I gave you more information than I should, so be grateful, especially after you brought *him* here. Iskaria made an unfortunate decision, and I fear the repercussions will impact all of us."

Ryker unclenched his hands. "If that's all, then we've taken up enough of your time."

Of course he'd be eager to leave.

"Yes, you all should be off." Elara gestured in the direction of the parked car. "The sooner you're off my property, the quicker I can try to forget I ever learned any of this information."

Raven chuckled harshly. "It's always the same with your kind, isn't it? So quick to dismiss the debts you owe, thinking your own interests supersede those of the people who have supported the witches through the centuries."

"The debts you claim I bear were created by my ancestors. Not me." Elara flushed. "My people have and will always come first. The vampire queen may have her own power, but at the end of the day, it's the well-being of my species that matters most to me."

Raven's teeth elongated, and her irises blurred crimson, evidence of her rising anger. "How noble. Yet you forget that, without our queen, you wouldn't be standing here today. The debt you owe is not just in coin or land but in loyalty. And loyalty, Elara, is something you seem to be sorely lacking. It has been noted."

"Make sure you put in bold that I stand with my sisters." Elara lifted her chin, unflinching at the clear threat that had been lobbed at her feet. "And I gave you more information than I wanted to, so please share that detail when you speak with the queen. Now it's time for the three of you to leave."

"Gladly," Ryker muttered, taking my hand and leading me back to the car. I glanced over my shoulder to see Raven and Elara still glaring at each other and even more fiercely with the two of us gone.

I dug my feet into the grass, wanting to stay and watch, but then they parted without another word. I had no clue what the stare-off meant, but my gut screamed that we needed to understand what the exchange was about. It seemed like more than just Elara not wanting to provide information to the vampires.

"We need to move, Ember," Ryker rasped and tugged on my hand. "Being here for as long as we have isn't good."

Yeah, I bet he felt that way. His touch didn't tingle, telling me the spell on him had activated once again. I sensed only a very minute hum.

I pivoted and picked up the pace to the car. Within two blinks of an eye, Raven was on my other side, slowing to keep pace with us.

She glared at Ryker, but he ignored her and opened the passenger door for me before climbing into the back seat behind me.

Raven slipped in her side, and the car's engine hummed to life. She pulled away from Elara's house, and soon, the expanse of the Shadowbrook Woods swallowed us whole. The faint glow of the dashboard, the headlights, and the rising moon were the only lights in the darkness.

That uncomfortable drowning sensation pressed on my body and had my heart racing. "I think the Blackwoods are near, or the witch is messing with my emotions," I gritted out, struggling to speak every word.

"How do you know?" Raven's head jerked my way, her eyes widening.

Ryker's sigh sounded like one of relief. Instead of Raven focusing on him, she wanted an explanation from me.

"I...I don't know. It's like... When they get close, I feel

a sort of cold pressure, and it's hard to breathe." That probably sounded crazy, but I wasn't sure how else to explain it.

"Well, I don't sense anything." Raven glanced from side to side, examining the forest. "If anything, it's Elara, just trying to get us off her property faster."

"I told you we shouldn't talk to witches," Ryker bit out, each word laced with disgust.

As if she'd been waiting for that opening, Raven said, "I think there's a more important reason than Elara using her magic to make us uncomfortable." Her voice cut through the car like a blade, sharp and precise. "So, Ryker, care to explain what she was talking about? The spell and the magic?"

"Luckily, I don't have to explain myself to you. All you need to know is that I *am* the same person, and my goals and loyalties haven't changed."

I grimaced, though I'd expected such a reaction from him. He'd clearly been trying to keep this magic a secret, and he was an alpha and didn't like to be questioned.

"You don't feel the need to explain yourself?" Raven's tone was calm but carried an undercurrent of frustration. "You've been acting strange for weeks, Ryker. Moody, unpredictable, volatile."

"What you should be worried about is that your heavily spelled protected area can't actually detect all magic." Ryker laughed harshly. "And I haven't been acting abnormal. I'm merely doing what needs to be done to get retribution for what the Blackwoods have done."

Silence filled the car, thick and oppressive, like a brewing storm. I tried to steady my breathing, but the lingering chill and pressure added to the tension, making my lungs even harder to fill.

Raven exhaled, her fingers drumming against the steering wheel. "We did know."

Ryker's breath caught. "You knew what?" His voice was flat, but I heard the trace of something dangerous.

My heart dropped into my stomach, and my mouth dried. The truth was finally coming out, and I might be caught in the cross fire since Raven had confided in me.

"That you were spelled." Raven flicked her eyes toward the rearview mirror. "We knew from the beginning. Our wards detected it when you arrived that day. They alerted me and Queen Ambrosia, and I wanted to give you a chance to come clean on your own first. To us. To your pack."

He snarled. "You think my pack doesn't know?"

Raven stilled. "Do they?"

"You assume I've been lying to them? We both know that's not possible."

"But withholding the truth works." Her tone turned frigid.

Ryker cracked his knuckles, a telltale sign of how close he was to losing his temper. I needed to intervene so Raven didn't take the brunt of his anger alone.

"Your pack doesn't know about the spell, but they've talked about how you've been acting more and more strangely. They believe it's from the burden you carry." I winced, thankful he couldn't see my expression. I had no doubt I looked strained. "What exactly did you think would happen, Ryker? That no one would notice?" He had to know that his packmates, the people who knew him almost as well as he knew himself, would realize something was off.

"I haven't changed," Ryker snarled. "I just want justice for our pack and yours."

That I understood, but we didn't have to lose our

humanity for vengeance. "You must have noticed that things change when you tap into that magic." I glanced over the headrest to stare into his eyes. The sheen covered the color once again. "Right now, there's an iridescent sheen over your eyes that's similar to how the shadows look to me."

His fingers curled into fists, his breathing shallow but controlled. "You don't understand—"

"Then help us understand," I urged, turning in my seat to face him fully. "Because right now, all I see is someone who made a deal involving magic without knowing the consequences."

He swallowed audibly, and a vein bulged between his eyebrows.

I gritted my teeth, ready for him to lash out and shut down the conversation entirely.

Instead, he said nothing.

The silence was louder than any denial could have been.

The uncomfortable cold seeped into my bones, pressing against me like a living force. My wolf whimpered as I spun around to face forward, needing to align my body in order to breathe.

The pressure grew stronger, constricting, suffocating. It was as if an invisible weight was crushing me into the seat, pinning me in place. My breath hitched, and my hands clenched on my thighs as I fought against it.

Something was wrong.

Very, *very* wrong.

I had felt this magic before.

"Ember?" Ryker's tone was anxious, his hand touching my shoulder as he leaned forward.

Raven glanced at me. "Is the witch using her magic on you?"

I shook my head as shadows emerged from the woods and surged forward from all directions, moving as quickly as the vehicle.

Dark tendrils slithered and coiled, racing toward us like a tide of living ink spilling across the ground.

"It's the Blackwoods," I rasped.

# CHAPTER SEVENTEEN

A vise wrapped around my heart, and it seemed to stop beating. We were *again* being attacked by our enemy, and this time, there were only three of us to defend ourselves. Even if we linked with our packs, they wouldn't get here in time to help.

Raven hissed and pressed harder on the gas. Gravel flew into the air and rattled under the car, leaving a huge dust trail behind us. "Fucking bastards. Can you tell how many?"

That was the problem. They all seemed to blend into one another before separating to reform into another sort of image. "A fuck ton is the only way I can describe it. Their bodies merge with one another in the shadows, so I can't make out individuals."

I rolled my neck, trying to release some of the compression. We'd be fighting within seconds. I couldn't be glued to the car seat, and I needed my body to adjust to the new environment like it had when we'd saved Briar.

"Fucking hell," Ryker snarled. "Go faster."

Raven's nostrils flared, and she stomped down even

harder, causing the tires to skid on the gravel just as the shadows swarmed us.

"They're—" Before I could finish that sentence, a high-pitched grating sound filled the vehicle, causing my eardrums to ache. They had to be running their claws against the windows, and the noise was more horrible than nails on a chalkboard. It was piercing to the point of being a screech while almost metallic.

When I thought it couldn't get worse, I was proven wrong once again.

A mix of sharp shrieks, low groans, and the occasional threatening thump sounded as something tried to rip through the car like a predator clawing at its prey. This had to be the echo of a nightmare.

Soon the tires began to thud as they lost air, leaving us with two choices—keep pushing and hope the rims held up, or get out and fight. The latter didn't seem like the best option.

Fate, being the bitch that she was, had the last laugh once again. If I'd had any doubts, this moment proved that she enjoyed watching me suffer.

The tires burst with deafening bangs, rubber tearing away in jagged strips that slapped against gravel. The vehicle hurtled into a frenzied skid, and the scenery blurred into obscurity as the shadows covered the windows.

The vehicle jerked violently to the left, and the seat belt dug into my shoulder as if the earth itself had tilted beneath us.

Raven's hands gripped the steering wheel, her knuckles pale against the leather. Her gaze darted between the road and the rearview mirror. "Hold on!" she yelled as the vehicle fishtailed, the back end swinging dangerously close to the trees before she expertly corrected the skid. But it was too late. The shadows had found their mark.

The car lurched and dropped to the ground as it careened out of control. I hit the front dashboard, and Ryker grabbed my shoulder and pulled me back against the seat as the world outside became a sea of sparks.

And then we rammed into the trunk of a large oak. My eyes closed as a scream lodged in my throat, but oblivion overtook me.

My eyes fluttered open, and the stench of copper assaulted my nose. Something didn't seem quite right, but I couldn't remember what it was. My head throbbed, and the faint tang of blood lingered on my lips, adding to the scent. I fidgeted, and my warm skin stuck to leather, contrasting with the faint moisture that seeped into my clothes.

Reality slammed into me. I tried to sit up, but a sharp pain shot through my temple.

"Ryker," I murmured despite my tongue feeling like sandpaper.

There was no response. I sensed the steady breathing and heartbeat of someone behind me and inhaled, trying like hell to smell him, but the stink of blood was too overpowering.

"I can't believe—" Raven's voice cut through the quiet.

"She's awake," a deep male voice cut her off.

I turned my head slowly, the huge oak trees casting long, ominous shadows across the clearing, but none that looked like the enemy.

Where had they all gone?

My door lay ripped off and crumpled about ten feet

from me. My arm throbbed, and I glanced at it to find deep claw marks oozing with blood. Whatever had done it had hit bone.

"Ember," Raven whispered, and my attention landed on her.

She stood in the center of the gravel road, blood streaking her usually flawless complexion. Her violet eyes glowed faintly in the darkness, and her clothes were torn and disheveled.

She was flanked by a pair of vampires, their faces pale and drawn, their eyes luminous in the night. Each of them bore signs of battle—cuts, scratches, and torn clothing that clung to their bodies. One of the vampires was leaning against a tree, their breathing shallow and labored, while the other knelt on the ground, a deep gash in their forearm that seemed to pulse with the faintest hint of crimson.

Behind them, a third vampire lay still, her body eerily pale and unresponsive. Her neck was slashed, and blood still oozed from the wound.

"Ryker?" I rasped, feeling as if knives were stabbing the back of my throat.

"He's alive and behind you," Raven answered as she and the two men hurried toward me. "I'm so glad you're okay."

I unbuckled the seat belt and snorted at the irony. My hands shook, and I clutched the side of the doorframe, trying to climb out of the vehicle. My arm throbbed all the way up to my shoulder.

"Let me help you." One of the new vampires, a caramel-haired man, rushed to my side. He slid his arm around my waist and helped me to my feet. I leaned all my weight on him because otherwise, I wouldn't be able to stand.

I needed to get to Ryker. I pivoted, the caramel-haired vampire not missing a beat and moving along with me. My throat tightened as my gaze landed on Ryker's unresponsive massive frame. Still, the slow rise and fall of his chest brought me comfort, though his face and arms had been clawed. One mark cut through the scab of his earlier wound as if done on purpose. Crimson covered one eye, and when he woke up, I had no doubt that it would feel as if it were on fire.

"What...what happened?" I coughed, the dryness in my throat unbearable. The way the caramel-haired man's hand lingered on my waist made my skin crawl. I tried to step away from him, but as soon as I placed my full weight on my feet, my knees gave out.

"Whoa." Caramel-haired guy grunted as he caught my waist again and pulled me tighter against him. "You need to be careful."

My wolf howled in protest from both not being able to get to Ryker and having another man's hands on me. Unfortunately, I knew better than to shove him away as my legs were shaking from holding so much of my weight, and the ground seemed to move underneath me.

"Here." Raven glided to my other side and placed her arm around me, allowing the caramel-haired man to release me.

As soon as he stepped away, my wolf calmed slightly, but the world kept spinning.

I'd lost too much blood, but I refused to sit down with Ryker unconscious and where the enemy could attack again at any second.

"When Queen Ambrosia learned Iskaria was missing, she called Lucinda to gather guards and follow us in case we ran into trouble." Raven shivered. "If they hadn't arrived..."

She trailed off, at a complete loss for words, which wasn't like her at all.

The other new vampire, a dark-haired man, smiled, but it seemed forced. "We arrived just as one dragged Raven from the car and two more were removing your and the other wolf's doors." His nose wrinkled a bit, but he smoothed it out. "Good thing the queen warned us. You're lucky—if that's what you call it."

Caramel-haired guy glanced at me with a furrowed brow. I smelled a brief waft of sweetness from the vampires before the strong stench and taste of blood overrode my senses again.

"The three of you managed to run them off?" I knew they were the queen's guards and probably some of the best warriors the vampires had, but there had to have been more than twenty attackers coming at us, given how they'd blended together. It could've been fifty or a hundred, for all I knew.

"The fiends thought they had us for sure." Raven shook her head. "Lucinda, Bella, and Martin have taken the other thirty guards that came with them to see if they can sense anything. They brought one of the relics a witch gave us to detect magic so they'll know if any is being used nearby. However, Foster"—she pointed at the caramel-haired man—"and David wanted to stay behind and help get you two back to safety as quickly as possible."

Vehicles. They had vehicles. Something we gravely needed.

"Where are the cars?" I blurted, my attention returning to Ryker. Once again, he was worse off than me, and he'd lost so much blood not even twenty-four hours ago. We had to leave *now*. "How far?" I scanned the area and saw a

Suburban about fifty yards away with about eleven matching black SUVs parked behind it.

David removed a key fob from his pocket and dangled it from his fingers. "I'll drive it down here. We stopped because we saw what was going on and we could reach you faster on foot." He jogged toward the first Suburban, leaving me with Raven and Foster. I stared at Ryker, his bloodied face searing into my mind.

My chest throbbed, and I wished I could take all his pain and suffering away. I understood that he'd kept something from me and the others, but I also understood the anger that kept festering in my own soul for the same reason as his.

"They're getting bolder." Foster's forehead creased with concern. "Attacking this close to vampire territory, taking a witch, and acting this close to another witch—they're either desperate or crazy."

I wished I could agree with that, but I didn't. "They're growing more confident."

"Which will make them reckless." Raven pressed her lips together. "We have to either determine how to track them or wait for them to make a mistake."

The SUV's engine started, and my gut hardened. The sound seemed to burst my eardrums, and a chill ran down my back. What if the attackers swung back around to finish us off?

No. I refused to become fearful. If I allowed them to influence my emotions, then they would win. No person, pack, or group would ever make me cower. I let out a sigh and pushed away the nagging fear that wanted to devour me. "But how many more people will die before that happens? And what if it doesn't?"

The vehicle zooming toward us came to a screeching

halt. David swung the door open and jumped out, leaving the engine running.

I scanned the area for any signs that something lurked nearby. Nothing seemed amiss, but the back of my neck prickled once again, signaling we were being watched.

The Blackwood witch had to be close. She was messing with my emotions right now. I bit the inside of my mouth, and more blood filled it, causing my stomach to roil in protest.

I moved toward Ryker and stumbled. I tried to catch myself, but my legs were jelly underneath me. Raven tried to catch me, but she, too, buckled under the pressure.

Moments before I would have hit the ground, Foster caught me. He pulled me to his chest, cradling me like a fucking princess, while David caught Raven by the arms. She whimpered, a sound I never expected to hear from her.

I tried to get out of Foster's arms to check on her and Ryker, but he held me tighter. "Nope. That's the second time you've almost fallen. Let me take you to the Suburban."

I wanted to climb out of my skin. Being in his arms felt so *wrong*. "I appreciate the help, but I'm fine."

Foster ignored me, tightening his hold even more. "You're not fine. Let's get you settled so we can get you three out of here."

Swallowing loudly, I bit back my protests. I clearly couldn't stand, and the world was spinning ever faster. Sitting down so I could rest and recover would be best and would allow them to focus on Ryker.

We had to stop his bleeding.

I shot a desperate look over Foster's shoulder as David got Raven back on her feet. She was paler than usual, her face almost as white as a sheet.

"Are you going to be okay?" I despised that I'd allowed her to help me when she was also so injured. Had I known, I would've fallen to the ground instead.

"I'll manage." She winced and clutched her arms to her sides. No doubt her injuries were similar to mine.

"Do you need help?" David arched a brow.

When Raven shook her head, he went to Ryker's side. He crouched and hesitated a moment before lifting him over his shoulder in a fireman's carry.

Ryker didn't stir, and fear gnawed at my insides. This was bad. Like he'd been the other day when he'd nearly died.

"See? They've got it covered." Foster began moving toward the vehicle, and suddenly I couldn't see Ryker any longer. Desperation froze my body.

I needed to watch to ensure a shadow didn't try to attack Ryker again...not when he was in this state.

I thrashed weakly, panic suffocating me. "Let's wait for them."

Foster's voice dripped with impatience. "You need to sit so you can start to heal."

"No," I yelled as my wolf surged forward, but I was too injured to shift. I *had* to watch to make sure Ryker wasn't attacked again, but Foster continued toward the vehicle, ignoring my protests.

A crash sounded behind us, followed by David's yelp of surprise.

Then a deep, guttural growl.

No. This couldn't be happening again.

CHAPTER EIGHTEEN

"L et her go," Ryker croaked, sounding weak but determined.

Foster spun around just as Ryker lifted himself up enough to wrap his arms around David's throat, flailing wildly.

David staggered, struggling to keep his grip on Ryker. With his free hand, he grabbed Ryker's hand, removing it from his neck. "Chill the fuck out. We're trying to help you," David rasped.

I had to get to Ryker. I had to stop this. My heart thundered against my rib cage. This wasn't going to end well if I didn't intervene.

"The fuck you are! Ember's trying to break free." Ryker lifted his arm, and I saw that his reopened knife wound had stained everything red. He didn't stop, muscles taut with distress. "Let her go, or I'll rip your throat out."

Foster rushed over so fast the wind blew my hair into my face. I relaxed in his grip, not wanting Ryker to hear me trying to get away anymore.

"Ryker, listen to me." The wind stopped, and we stood

only a few feet from Ryker. His gaze found mine, one eye covered by the blood running down his face. He blinked, and I had no doubt that he was hurting. I continued, "I'm okay. I just wanted to be put down. You're hurt. Please— look at me."

Ryker's wild look softened, and he stopped fighting David. His grip on the vampire loosened, and he took a shaky breath and grimaced. His attention remained on me.

Finally, maybe we could get him calm and try to stop the bleeding. I took a deep breath...then anger sparked in Ryker's eyes.

"Do *not* touch her," he seethed. He straightened and pressed his hands on David's shoulder then dropped to his feet.

"What the—" David muttered.

Ryker took an unsteady step toward me.

"Let me down." I fought again to get free, and the iridescent sheen covered Ryker's irises once again. I turned and whispered to Foster, so low that no one else could hear in the chaos, "It's for your own good."

"But you can't—" Foster started.

"You heard her," Raven said, her voice echoing in the clearing. "Put her down *now*." She appeared between Ryker and us, blocking Ryker from me.

Ryker took another step, but his legs were shaking. Blood dripped from his reopened wound. He staggered, pain etched deep into his features. "Get your hands *off* her."

"Listen to her *now*," Raven repeated. She moved to my side, her gaze steady as Foster lowered me to the ground. Then she wrapped an arm around me.

My stomach knotted. Even though I appreciated what Raven was doing, I didn't need or want her help either. I'd find the strength to stand on my own, or I'd damn well crawl to the vehicle. Anything to get Ryker calmed enough to get care. "You're hurt—"

"Not like you two are." Raven shook her head. "I'll be fine."

"Let me help too," Foster insisted, but before he could touch me, both Raven and I moved so that all his hands caught was air.

Ryker snarled and tried to lunge; however, it was more of a stumble. "Get away from her, or I'll *kill* you."

"But—" Foster flinched.

"We're fine," Raven spat. "You've done enough for the night. I'll take it from here."

He lifted both hands, which were now coated in my blood. "Understood." Then he stepped away.

The tension flowed out of Ryker's body, and he tried to step toward me again. "Lil rebel," he breathed.

I tried to go toward him, but my knees buckled. Despite being mere feet from each other, we might as well have been miles apart.

"For Fate's sake." David rolled his eyes. "All three of you are a mess. It's only going to get worse if we don't get you back to the mansion and tended to."

Ryker swayed dangerously, and David barely caught him before he hit the ground.

"I'm okay." Somehow, I understood that he needed to reach me as much as I did him. The urge to get to him had me damn near frantic to just touch him. "Let's get in the vehicle so we can go back to our pack."

He wiped the eye covered with crimson, and his face twisted in agony. "Only if you stay beside me."

That wasn't a hard ask. "Agreed."

David reached for Ryker again, but he shook his head. "I will *not* be carried." When Foster moved in my direction,

Ryker turned toward him and snarled, "And you don't get near her again."

I had to mash my lips together to prevent myself from laughing. Even severely injured, Ryker refused to be carried by a male vampire. That sounded about right. His wolf wouldn't allow his ego to be challenged and didn't want anyone who was viewed as a potential threat near me.

"I'll help her." Raven moved forward.

Slowly, I moved in tandem with her, and David supported a part of Ryker's arm that didn't have any wounds to assist him.

The five of us finally made it to the vehicle, and a lump formed in my throat.

Briar.

If over fifty vampires had come here to help us, that meant the mansion wasn't heavily guarded right now.

*Are you okay?* I linked, tugging on our pack connection. As the pack alpha, I could feel her emotions a lot more than when I'd been just a member of the pack. Nothing seemed out of sorts other than the concern she'd felt when we left, and our connection was warm, meaning she was awake. Still, I needed to talk with her.

She answered immediately. *Yeah, are you? I've been worried sick, but I didn't want to ask and distract you if you were in the middle of a situation.*

That was something Dad had howled into our ears our entire childhood. When we knew he was going to attend a meeting, we were not to interrupt unless it was a life-and-death situation. I used to think he was being dramatic, but now, thanks to having to handle true life-and-death situations, I understood. It wasn't just having conversations; I was strategizing and having to evaluate word choice, motivations, and body language for clues.

I told her about the first witch going missing, most likely abducted, and then what had happened with the second witch just now.

*What? Fifty vampire guards left here, and they didn't tell us you were in danger?* The heat of her anger pulsed through our connection. *And you and Ryker didn't alert us about it either?*

Guilt sat heavy in my stomach. Reaching out to her hadn't even crossed my mind. But now I realized why—I didn't want her to be in danger when we were so outnumbered. *You're fifteen minutes away. You wouldn't have gotten here in time, and there were easily over twenty attackers.*

*How would you feel if I were in that situation and I didn't contact you?*

I cringed so hard that the pain shot through my head once again, making me gasp. She had a point, and I didn't want to admit it to her. So instead, I tried the only option I had left. *Ryker is severely injured. He needs food and hydration. Can you work on that for him? His old wound has reopened, and he has cuts all over his face and arms. And I'm sure Raven needs blood. She's hurt too, but not as bad as Ryker.*

Ryker's breath came unevenly, and his steps faltered. The world around me spun even faster. Even a Tilt-A-Whirl ride didn't make me feel this dizzy.

*What about you?*

We reached the vehicle, and Foster opened the back door. I gripped the car roof and pulled myself into the vehicle. Sweat beaded on my forehead, but I persevered, getting into the back seat.

*Ember,* Briar exclaimed, pulling me back into the present. *Are you hurt?*

My initial impulse was to tell her no, but then she'd be even more pissed when we arrived at the mansion.

"I'm getting in the back seat with her," Ryker rasped as he slowly lifted himself into the vehicle. I noticed David was assisting a little without trying to be too obvious.

*I'm injured, but I'll be okay.* I had to be. I just needed to eat something and rest, and then my wolf-shifter healing would kick in.

Ryker slumped beside me, laying his head on the back of the bench seat with his face turned toward me, so close that his breath caressed my skin.

*How bad?* Briar insisted.

Unfortunately, she knew how I operated, which didn't bode well for me.

Raven got into the middle-row seat behind Foster while David slid into the driver's seat. Foster typed something on his phone as David pulled onto the road, heading back to safety.

*I need to eat and rest too.* I bit my bottom lip, ready for the explosion.

*Ember Sinclair. How could you not tell me?* Her concern constricted the bond. *We're a pack and family!*

I winced at the intensity of her emotions. I had hurt her again. However, I was drained and didn't have the energy to argue with her. *I'm sorry. But I'm exhausted and hurting. Can we please talk about it tomorrow?*

She paused like she was battling with herself over whether to respect my wishes or let loose some of her frustration.

Luckily, I knew what that meant. She would cave. She cared so much about the people she loved, and sometimes, I wished I were more like her. If I were in her position, I wouldn't stop lecturing me.

*Fine. But only because I love you and care about your well-being. Tomorrow, we're going to have this discussion. You're not getting out of it.*

She used to threaten that but then relent. Not this time; something inside me understood that she was going to follow through. After our pack had been killed, not only had I changed, but Briar had too, and she'd clearly grown a backbone. *Thank you. And I love you too, baby wolf.* I used Dad's term of endearment for her.

Ryker's breathing became shallow, and his chest rose and fell faster than normal. Blood began congealing on his face and arms, but his side remained bright red. He was still bleeding. My wolf whimpered, and my blood froze. He moved a little and placed his head on my shoulder as he snored.

My arm ached where his body pressed against claw marks. Still, he was resting, and there was no way in hell I would move and risk disturbing him.

I had one last concern. "Should we not wait for the other vampires?" I felt bad leaving them behind.

"No." Raven glanced over her shoulder. "Lucinda and the others know we're heading back to the mansion. There's plenty of room for all the vampires in the rest of the vehicles. They'll call me if something concerning happens."

That was more than fine with me. Lucinda hated us, so the farther away we were from one another, the better.

I listened to Ryker's heartbeat, letting my thoughts race. The witch's warning about the spell cast upon him echoed in my mind. Acid burned my throat, and cold sweat pooled in my armpits. I had to get answers from him, and I hated that he'd kept so much from me and his pack members. Everything had to be addressed, but we first had to heal.

The discomfort in my arm intensified, and nausea

swirled in my stomach in sync with the world around me. I tried staring out the window, but all that accomplished was making me gag.

Between the silence, the stench of blood, and the strained atmosphere, the car ride seemed unending. But eventually, we pulled up to the mansion and stopped in front of the Queen Ambrosia statue.

Even before David put the car in park, Gage and Kendric raced out the front door toward us. Gage's usual smile was gone, replaced by a deep scowl. If I'd thought Gage's expression was concerning, that changed when my attention landed on Kendric.

With a body so tense I wasn't sure how he could move and his nostrils flaring, Kendric looked ready to go to war. The two of them hurried to the passenger door and yanked it open.

When Kendric saw Raven, his expression softened. "Are you okay?" He placed his hands gently on her arms.

"I'm fine. Ryker and Ember are way worse off than me."

"You better be glad you let the queen know what was going on and she had us come for backup," David interjected.

Kendric's face hardened, and he glanced in the back seat at Ryker and me. His nostrils flared. "You took the time to inform the queen?"

"Kendric, I—" Raven started as she climbed out of the vehicle and stood before him.

"You need to *move*," he bit out. "Gage and I will help Ember and Ryker inside to be taken care of."

For the first time, I saw Raven sag. The confidence she always carried vanished before my eyes at the words of the man she clearly loved. "Listen—"

He moved past her and climbed into the vehicle, not

looking back or acknowledging her. When he looked over Ryker and me, his expression strained.

Foster and David told Raven they were heading inside to check in with the other guards. Their footsteps grew quieter as they walked away.

"How bad off is he?" Kendric asked softly as if he was afraid of bothering Ryker.

I licked my lips, trying to wet my dry mouth. "He's lost a lot of blood. He needs calories and rest."

"Briar is taking care of that." Kendric's large form was cramped in the small opening. "Here, let's get you out first." He gently lifted Ryker's head from my shoulder then moved so I could get out.

Gage leaned in to support some of my weight. Once I was out, he lifted me into his arms and waited outside the car.

Once again, my skin crawled, but not as bad as it had with Foster.

Gage examined my face and smirked, coming off like the friend I knew. He chuckled. "I always knew that one day I would sweep you off your feet." He waggled his brows.

Despite my dizziness, I managed to note his reaction. I snorted. "That was super cheesy."

"Yes, but it got a smile out of you, which was the goal." He winked.

A little bit of anxiety unwound in my chest, and soon, Kendric came out with Ryker in his arms, carried like a princess. As soon as Kendric was out of the car, Raven was at his side.

She opened her mouth, but Kendric strode past her to Gage, and we headed inside. Raven followed us through the house, her footsteps soft and deliberate.

Within seconds, we entered the bedroom, where a pale-faced Briar stood by Ryker's bed, holding two red Solo cups. The mattress was covered in a thick white comforter to protect it from bloodstains.

I could only assume they used white so they could bleach it when we were done with them.

"Put them both here," Briar commanded, urgency in her voice as she gestured to the bed.

The two men obeyed, Gage settling me on the side closest to my sister. My head spun, but Briar handed one cup to Gage while she pressed the straw of the other to my lips. "Drink this."

The potent scent of nutrients wafted from it—protein powder, sugar, electrolytes. I took a huge gulp, the liquid coating my throat and washing away the taste of blood.

I glanced at Ryker, who drank as he slept. No doubt the influence of his wolf wanting to heal.

A huge sigh left me. Maybe he'd be okay.

"Kendric, I know you're upset." Raven bit her lip. "But—"

Kendric spun around, his normally calm eyes blazing. He snarled, "Are you sure you want to do this now?"

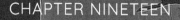

## CHAPTER NINETEEN

The last thing we needed was more drama and heartbreak. Everyone had been on edge, but for the past thirty-six hours, our situation seemed to have gotten worse and worse. The Blackwoods were attacking us both mentally and physically, and they were succeeding in getting us to turn on one another.

I opened my mouth to say something, but I wasn't fast enough.

"I don't understand why you're so upset with me." Raven blinked, the flash of pain on her face almost too quick to catch.

Clenching his hands into fists, Kendric growled. "I'm not sure what you don't understand. You had time to contact Ambrosia and coordinate a rescue with her guards, but not to inform me that the three of you were in danger?"

Shit. Raven didn't deserve all the blame. That fell just as much on Ryker and me.

Raven stumbled back as if she'd been struck. "We didn't know what we were getting into," she said quietly. "I didn't think we'd be attacked. And I—"

"You didn't think you might be attacked after discovering a witch was missing?" Kendric shook his head. "We deserved to know this information just as soon as the vampires did. All it would have taken was a quick text."

She opened her mouth then closed it, her silence cutting deeper than words.

I sucked in a breath, ignoring the way my head ached. "Raven's not the one to blame here. If you're going to be mad at anyone, it should be me."

Raising a hand, Kendric pivoted so he could see both Raven and me. "Ember, I know what you're doing, and it's not helping. Yes, you and Ryker should've linked with us. Don't worry. Xander, Gage, Briar, and I are pissed at both of you as well, and when the two of you are better, it *will* be addressed. But Raven not including me in her communication is starkly different. She's supposed to be my partner and equal, unlike Ryker, who's my alpha. However, this event showed me the truth. Clearly, I am *way* more invested than she is, and it's all one-sided."

I flinched, the pounding in my head increasing. The room spun faster as the edge of my vision began to darken, and I slumped back onto the pillow.

"Dammit, Ember." Briar *tsk*ed, sounding just like our mother. "You've got to drink as much as you can now before you pass out." She jabbed the straw between my lips, but the idea of drinking made me want to vomit.

My wolf leaped forward, survival instincts kicking in. I took a long sip, the taste of powdered protein and something overly sweet filling my mouth. I swallowed another huge swig, hoping it would settle my stomach.

A storm of emotions flickered within Raven's eyes. "Kendric, you know if I could've told you, I would."

"What does that even mean? Why couldn't you? Aren't

we allies? Aren't I your fucking boyfriend?" His voice broke, dripping with hurt. "I made sure to keep you informed of everything."

I closed my eyes, hating that I couldn't fix this.

"The queen told me she'd handle the situation." Raven's voice was strained. "I didn't know this would happen. You must see that."

"Did she tell you not to alert me and the pack?" he challenged.

*Hey, it's going to be okay,* Briar linked and ran a hand through my tangled hair. *Kendric and Raven's disagreement isn't your fault.*

If I weren't feeling so awful, I'd laugh. My sister knew me better than I knew myself.

I took another big mouthful, knowing it'd be my last. My wolf settled, and the strange new warm feeling within me began to pulse throughout my body.

*Get some rest. You're going to need it when you wake up and I get hold of you.*

Warm, firm lips pressed against my forehead, I heard the door open and shut, and then the room became silent. I peeked out. Both Kendric's huge, looming figure and Raven's tall, slender frame were gone. They must have taken their argument somewhere else, and I hated that I couldn't have Raven's back like she'd had ours.

"Ember..." Ryker mumbled and groaned.

Instinctively, I found his hand and squeezed, ignoring the sharp pain that traveled up my arm. "I'm right here. We're safe for now." The buzz of our connection sprang up between us, releasing some of the worry that had settled on my shoulders. When he had been near death, it became almost too faint to feel.

He moved, and I looked over and saw that he'd turned

his face in my direction. I wanted to stare into his eyes and rejoice that he seemed better off than I'd feared, but the world turned too quickly for me to maintain eye contact.

"Stay beside me, please."

"Always" left my lips before I even processed what I'd said.

But before I could, sleep overtook me.

---

Something tugged at my consciousness, and I became aware of a soft sound—a steady and strong heartbeat. My eyes fluttered open to find Ryker watching me, his expression intent yet tender. The warmth of his gaze sent a different kind of pulse through me, tingling beneath my skin. My wolf edged forward.

He exhaled, tucking a loose strand of hair behind my ear. "How are you feeling?"

The intimate touch had my face warming, and I managed a weak smile. "Like I got hit by three trucks and dragged for miles. I'm exhausted." I yawned, unable to hold it back. However, when I lifted my head, it gave only a twinge of discomfort. "How about you?"

An amused glint sparked the golden tinges in his hazel eyes. "Well, if you got hit by three trucks, then I'm going to say two. There's no way you'll outheal me, lil rebel."

Before I could protest, he pulled me gently into his arms.

"Your injuries." My gaze flicked to his stomach. The bandage had been changed and was stark white again, and his arms seemed to have been cleaned and had already scabbed over, which shouldn't have been possible even with wolf-shifter healing.

"Don't worry. I'm truly feeling a lot better than last night."

Without a good reason not to, my body moved in sync with his as if it were the most natural thing in the world. He nestled my head against his shoulder, and I breathed in his scent, earthy and warm. We stayed that way, our closeness soothing and charged at once.

His chest rumbled. "I never thought I'd get to hold you like this."

The room spun again, though not from blood loss and pain this time. "I really didn't think we'd make it out of there."

"But we did." He leaned his head against mine.

*I'll be in there with breakfast for you two soon,* Briar linked. *I'm assuming you both need your bandages changed and another protein drink.*

My stomach grumbled at the thought. However, something more substantial would be nice. *How about a steak?*

*A steak?* Her shock blasted through our connection. *I don't think that's wise since you struggled with drinking a quarter of the protein mixture I made for you last night.*

*Mixture is right.* I wanted to vomit just thinking about the awfulness, but to her credit, I did feel much better. "Briar is making us something to eat. Do you want a steak?"

His brows lifted comically. "Fuck yeah. My mouth is already drooling just thinking about it."

*Make that two steaks, please.* Normally, I was the one in the kitchen cooking and baking. Wistfulness took me by surprise. In all the chaos, I had barely gotten to bake except for some brownies while we were at the vampire mansion, something I'd done daily until the night of the ceremony.

For the first time, thinking of Reid's rejection didn't

make me ache. Instead, I could breathe better and relief washed over me.

*Are you sure?*

*Yes, we're starving. Whatever you gave us last night made us crave something to help our wolf sides heal better.*

After a pause, she replied, *I don't think it's a good idea. I'll make the steaks because I know someone will eat them if you two don't, but I'm bringing you the drink too. I have no doubt you'll change your mind.*

Ryker turned fully toward me and placed a finger under my chin, lifting my face to his. His gaze darted to my lips, and my wolf howled with anticipation as my stomach fluttered. As he leaned his head down to mine, I placed a hand on his chest, stopping him.

His eyes widened a little before his expression fell. "Are you still determined to fight what's between us even after both of us almost died last night?"

Guilt knotted deep inside me. He was right; we'd almost lost each other last night, but that didn't make things suddenly okay. "What I feel for you isn't the problem." My voice was more forlorn than I intended.

"If this is about that fucking vampire, then I don't know what to say. I did what had to be done."

My temper flared. "He was an *innocent*. You can't just attack people like that."

"Ember, he wasn't an innocent." He closed his eyes for a moment and exhaled. "I know he wasn't."

I rolled my eyes and moved back a little despite my wolf and body protesting. "Do you think I'm stupid? I know what I saw! He was hiding from the attackers and witnessed his entire nest dying in front of him."

"I know because of the magic that was placed on me,"

Ryker huffed. "I can see people's souls and read what type of person they are."

I blinked. I hadn't seen that coming. "So what had he done?"

His irises turned a more vivid brown. "I don't know. I can only tell what type of person he is. But I promise you, I've never tortured someone who was a *good* person."

For some reason, this sat worse with me instead of better. I pulled away even more.

"Are you seriously pissed because you were wrong about Simon being a good person?"

I bit the back of my bottom lip, scraping off a scab and causing blood to fill my mouth. Afraid of what I might say next, I shook my head.

"Then what's the problem?" His tone was sharp.

I hesitated, the truth sticking in my throat like a knife. For the first time ever, I didn't want to say the words because it would confirm that it was true. He was officially making me doubt my own sanity. Finally, I forced it out. "You proved what I always knew. I can't trust you."

Ryker's face flushed. "What the hell does that mean?"

My chest tightened as anger and frustration crashed inside me. "It means you're only coming clean now because you were found out."

He ran a hand down his face and grimaced. "That's not fair. When I found you that day and pulled you out of the water, we didn't like or want to be around each other. It wasn't one-sided; it was mutual, so when exactly was I supposed to tell you? We've been in constant danger, and you're fighting our connection so damn hard."

"Why shouldn't I fight it? Feeling anything for someone outside of my pack hasn't worked out well for me." The words tore from me, leaving me bare in front of him. "I got rejected by my fated mate, remember? You were there."

Ryker's face twisted into pure rage. He grabbed my wrists and pinned me beneath him. His grip was firm but not painful, trapping me against the bed.

My breath caught.

"You better *never*," he snarled and leaned close to my ear, "*ever* refer to Reid as your fated mate again."

His voice reverberated through me, leaving shock in its wake. Instead of rallying against the male holding us down, my wolf surged toward him with wild abandon. I gasped, my chest heaving, as I realized that part of me really wanted this.

He didn't let go. Instead, he leaned closer, his scent enveloping me until it was all I could breathe. "You're mine, Ember." The words were possessive, a declaration. His eyes locked with mine, and he lifted his chin in a challenge.

I wanted to get lost in him and throw caution to the wind. But I couldn't. Not with both of us being alphas and the repercussions that could happen with two alphas merging and sorting all that out while going into battle. Not when he'd kept something so important from me, and I sensed there was more. "You're still not telling me everything, Ryker. I don't even know what's going on anymore."

His grip shifted, and he released my wrists, but the weight of his stare didn't lessen. "Have *you* told *me* everything?"

My heart stuttered. "What's that supposed to mean?"

"Exactly what it sounds like." He crossed his arms. "Can you say you've been completely honest with me? Or even with your sister? Because I suspect you've not told her everything either."

I swallowed hard, the cold accusation curling around

my own fears. I couldn't speak because I had to tell the truth, or he'd know I was lying.

I didn't want to play games with him anymore. I was tired.

He scowled, and his shoulders sagged like he was disappointed. "So you're keeping things from me as well and getting pissed because I've done the same thing. Isn't that hypocritical?" He pushed off the bed, frustration rippling through him as he raked a hand through his hair. He placed a hand on the bandage at his waist, evidence that he wasn't as healed as he tried to pretend. "You're so stubborn. You want to be angry at me when you're doing the same damn thing." He pivoted toward me, his face lined with pain. "So what are *you* hiding?"

My throat tightened. "I—I don't want to do this right now."

"I told you how I knew Simon wasn't a good person." He leveled a finger at me. "Now it's your turn to reveal what you're hiding from me."

The words burned on my lips, and I realized I had to come clean. No matter how hard it was. "Fine." I blew out a breath and sat up, my body aching from my injuries. "I knew about the spell that was placed on you before we went to the witch's house."

His jaw dropped. "What? How?"

I swallowed. "Each time your magic triggers, I see an iridescent glow cover your irises. I was confused and didn't understand it, but then Raven discussed it with me before we left to retrieve Briar. She told me that you'd been spelled but that you hadn't confided in anyone, including your own pack."

His expression crumpled into something raw and unguarded. "That was just a few days ago...after the new vampire attacked you in the woods." His voice was hoarse, his tone accusatory.

Pain lanced through me, sharper than any physical wound. It was the first time he'd looked at me that way—like I'd betrayed him. "I had to agree to keep it a secret before she told me. I didn't know what she wanted to tell me, but..." I stopped, realizing I was digging myself deeper into the hole.

"And you still didn't feel like you should say anything? After everything we'd been through together? She told you after we started connecting. At least, my secret was from before we started trusting one another."

He was right. I was a complete and utter hypocrite. "I wasn't trying to hide my knowing about it from you." I hated the way my voice broke. I sounded weak. "I just—I wanted to figure out what it meant before I told you."

"Sure. Whatever makes you feel better at night." He headed for the door. "I'm going to see if the steaks are done."

No. I couldn't let him leave—not like this.

I jumped to my feet and raced to him, ignoring my body's protests. As he reached the handle, I grabbed his hand, turning him toward me. "Wait. Please."

# CHAPTER TWENTY

My wolf whimpered, and my vision blurred. We'd had disagreements before, but this one was different. I wasn't quite sure why, but I wanted a chance to fully explain myself. He was right that both of us had been wrong.

He dropped his hand and stepped toward me once again.

Silence enveloped us, and my mind raced as I tried to determine how to begin. This moment would define everything, including whether I lost him.

He was opening his mouth when Briar opened the door.

She juggled two plates and had two large cups with straws clutched between her arms and chest. She stopped in her tracks when she noticed us standing there. "Oh! I was bringing your food in here. I didn't expect..." She trailed off.

Ryker kept his gaze locked on me, but when I didn't say anything, he let out a shaky breath. "I can eat just fine in the kitchen." He took a plate and drink from her and headed out the door.

The weight of what just happened pressed heavily on me, and I felt as if I were suffocating.

When the door shut, Briar turned to me, eyes wide. "Ember?"

I blinked, trying to hold back tears and pull myself together. I forced a smile, making my cheeks hurt. "Thank you so much for the food." I took the other plate and drink from her and headed back to the bed. I sat on the edge of the mattress near the end table, where the sheet was clean of blood.

As I placed the plate and drink on the table and grabbed the knife, she sat on Gage's bed directly across from me.

She leaned forward, placing her elbows on her knees. "What just happened? You don't have to pretend with me."

I picked at the food, my appetite gone. "Everything's just...complicated. But it'll be fine." The words sounded hollow, even to me. "Our focus has to be on finding evidence to get all the packs to work together to take down the Blackwoods. We're not going to be able to do it alone. Thank Fate the vampires are on our side, or Raven, Ryker, and I would've died last night."

"Speaking of which, I'm not happy with you about that." Briar crossed her arms and glared. "I get that you're my alpha, but you're still my sister and the only family and pack member I have left. I should've been informed, at the very least. Put yourself in my paws."

She might as well have punched me in the gut. Once again, I hadn't made the right call. What an amazing alpha I was turning out to be. "You're right. I'm sorry. Being the older sister and alpha, my gut instinct is to protect you. But you're an adult, and I should treat you like such. After all, you're my beta." I cut a piece of steak off, noting that it was medium rare. Still, my stomach wasn't enthusiastic like it had been ten minutes ago. I placed the fork and knife down and dropped my hands into my lap.

"Okay then." She pursed her lips. "I wasn't expecting you to agree that easily. And I'm your beta by default." She stuck her tongue out but then placed a hand over mine. "I'm assuming this feeds into your argument with Ryker."

I toyed with the straw in the cup. "Partly."

She straightened, concern etched on her face. "What's going on?"

I wanted to loop her in, but it wasn't only my story to share. "All I can say is that I know something he's kept secret from his own pack. I wish I could tell you more. I want to, but it's not my place."

Laughing, she tilted her head back. "Why is he so upset if he's the one keeping secrets? What right does he have? It sounds like he's taking it out on you."

"He's not the only..." The temptation to just agree with her was there. I did believe he was taking out some of his frustration at being caught on me, but he wasn't the only one in the wrong. Something I had to see and admit, even if I didn't want to.

All mirth vanished from her face. "What do you mean?"

"I'm doing the same to all of you," I replied softly, feeling the sting of my admission.

She blinked. "So...both of you are being hypocrites. What haven't you told me?"

That was the problem. I couldn't tell her without ratting him out. My head bowed, feeling the weight of everything even more. "He called me out just before you came in."

"What are you going to do?"

I rubbed my temples, trying to quell the renewed pounding there. "I don't know. Yes, I kept something from him, but it was only because the thing I found out was what he was trying to keep from us." For a second, I felt like I was back in high school.

She leaned over and squeezed my hand before letting go. "Well, it's a damn good thing you have me. You're not alone this time. I'm here, and we'll figure all of it out together."

That did provide comfort, but my wolf and heart still ached. I stared at the food without touching it.

Briar picked up my fork. "You need to eat."

I sighed and took the utensil from her then ate a bite of warm steak.

"You're lucky you didn't die of blood loss." She crossed her legs and watched. "Maybe you want to starve yourself because you feel as if you did something horrible, but you're not allowed to do that when lives are on the line."

The meat lodged in my throat, so I took a sip of the putrid drink she'd made me. It washed the steak down, but the combination tasted like ass on my tongue. Still, the one forkful had my appetite slowly returning, even though the knot in my stomach was still there.

Right now, I had to focus on getting better and figuring out our next steps. There were hundreds, if not thousands, of lives at stake. I didn't have time to figure out a man who kept things from the people closest to him.

So I tried like hell to push him out of my thoughts and heal.

Three days passed, during which Ryker and Kendric avoided the house like the plague, staying in the woods to help the vampires guard the perimeter.

Gage told me that Ryker had informed their pack about

the spell placed on him, and it had caused a divide and a ton of tension among them.

Each night that Ryker and Kendric didn't return caused my heart to splinter more. The only comfort was that Gage, Xander, and Briar were with me, so I didn't feel alone.

However, I didn't have time to focus on Ryker doing everything he could to avoid coming back to help us. He'd been keeping in touch with Gage and Xander, giving them updates, and they returned the favor begrudgingly.

The two of them, Briar, Raven, and I, were in the study, surrounded by ancient books, maps, and a laptop on the long oak table. We were trying to pinpoint where additional witches who might provide us with information might be.

Briar tapped her pen against her notepad. "I don't get it. It's like these witches just disappear into thin air."

Across from me, Raven typed on the laptop, her fingers dancing across the keyboard. She leaned back in her chair and steepled her fingers. "That may be exactly what they are doing. There are several remote locations historically known for witch activity." She paused, eyes flicking toward me. "During times of unrest, it's common for them to retreat, especially if they sense danger or seek to avoid getting entangled in power struggles."

"They're out there, but they won't be easy to find."

Gage snorted from his spot to my right and said, "Yeah, or maybe they just want to keep everyone in the dark and avoid answering inconvenient questions. I understand that strategy well enough." He glanced at Xander, on my other side, and gave him a smart-ass smile.

I flinched. Even though I was still upset with Ryker, I understood why he'd done it. He'd been misguided, but we were all doing the best we could.

Raven continued as if she hadn't heard him. "They

might know more about the attacks and Ryker's condition than we realize. But I must warn you—approaching them will not be easy. Trust is not given lightly in their circles."

I sighed, pushing a map aside. "Well, it won't be an issue unless we can find one. We should focus on pinpointing a location before worrying about how we'll approach them."

Xander dragged a hand through his hair, leaning over the table. "Then where do we start? We've been searching for days, and they're like ghosts."

"Good one, man." Gage gave a thumbs-up. "I'm down with puns."

I bit my bottom lip, trying to hide the grin that wanted to spread across my face. Even though the situation seemed dire, Gage had a way of lightening things up.

Blinking, Xander tilted his head back. "What are you talking about?"

"Ghosts, bruh." Gage patted his chest. "I dig it."

"Not following, man." Xander's face smushed into confusion.

"Dear Fate." Briar dropped her pen on the notebook. "Ghosts can't be seen. Blackwoods are being cloaked."

"That's not even funny." Xander blew out a breath.

Raven cleared her throat, trying to get us back on topic. "Elara mentioned that the witch performing the cloaking spell would have to be staying near the Blackwoods."

"The Blackwoods' territory is massive, and we can't be sure she's actually on their land." Every time we tried to get ahead of them, we wound up falling several feet behind.

I wanted to scream in frustration. "If they're working with more witches, we might be looking in the wrong places. We have no idea who their allies are. It could be other wolf packs for all we know."

Briar braced both hands on the table. "Would they have more than one working with them? Surely not."

I clenched my teeth. "We can't keep going in circles like this. Each minute that passes is a minute closer to another attack."

Gage opened his mouth, but Raven's phone rang, silencing him.

She glanced at the screen and then placed it to her ear quickly. "Yes?" Her dark eyes widened slightly before she held it out in my direction. "It's for you, Ember. It's Bruce."

I grabbed it and held it to my ear. "Bruce?"

The familiar voice, smooth and low, came through the line. "We've got something, Ember. We've been watching the Blackwoods' perimeter, keeping tabs on any unusual activity."

My heart leaped at the urgency in his tone. "Okay. Did you find something?"

"Two pack members mentioned they saw a witch leave the property. A car came by and picked her up." I heard a pause and then some rustling as he seemed to be moving. "She wasn't carrying anything, so we're hoping she'll be back soon. Maybe a run to get herbs or something for a potion."

My chest expanded with hope. Maybe we finally had a breakthrough. I gripped the phone tightly. "Can you let us know if she returns? We'll get ready in case we need to move." Luckily, the mansion was only about twenty minutes from Blackwood territory.

"Will do. Keep the phone close. More of us are heading that way since we have a longer drive."

It was a good call. If we had to attack, we'd want as many hands on deck as possible. "Don't take too many people. We don't want them alerted in case they're watching."

The click of a door closing sounded on the other side of the line. "We'll keep it small. I'll be in touch once we have more news."

The phone went dead, and I lowered it to see everyone staring with wide eyes, excitement practically vibrating off them.

"They spotted a witch leaving the Blackwoods' territory. There's a chance she's running an errand and will come back soon."

Gage pumped a fist in the air while Xander let out a low whistle.

"Can you link with Ryker?" My wolf ached as I spoke, desperate to see him. "Let him know what's going on?" It was a good thing that I couldn't pack-link with him because I might have tried to talk to him despite our needing space from one another.

"Do we have to?" Gage pouted. "He might find her and not tell anyone. I trust you more than him."

The words were a slap in the face. I'd kept something from them too, but if I had shared, then Ryker's spell would've been outed by me. "Yes, we need him." The words were both hard and easy to say. Ryker was one of the strongest wolves out there, and we needed our best to be involved.

Xander's eyes glowed. "I just informed him and Kendric —they're on their way back now."

"The four of you should meet with them and resolve this issue before we try to locate the witch." Raven stood and smoothed her tunic over her black pants. "Like Ember said, we won't be able to take a massive group, so we need to be able to operate well with each other. I'll talk with

Lucinda and the others and coordinate the group from our side."

My mouth dried. She was right. We all had to talk, but I wasn't sure that this problem could be fixed in the time we had. This issue was one of massive betrayal and lack of trust.

We all exited the study, leaving the laptop and maps scattered across the table. Raven headed out the front door, and Briar's footsteps padded right behind me.

*Raven's right. It's imperative we get on the same side before we head out. I'll talk to Ryker first so we can determine how to solidify the group. Can you distract Xander and Gage so they don't follow me outside?* Even though all that was true, I also needed to see how bad things were between Ryker and me. I didn't want to figure that out with an audience.

She nodded and gave my arm a comforting squeeze. *I got you, sis.*

As I stepped into the backyard, the cool mountain air hit my face, and my wolf grew restless. We hadn't shifted in days, and she wanted to be free. However, I hadn't wanted to risk running into Ryker while he wanted distance from me.

The sounds of leaves crunching had me looking to the right, and Kendric stepped out of the trees. Twigs stuck out of his dark hair, and his mouth was set in a deep frown. He slowed down to speak, but I wanted him gone before Ryker got here. I had to talk to Ryker alone.

"I'll be in shortly with Ryker." I stood straight, trying to appear more confident than the trembling mess I was inside. "I need to talk to him."

His eyes flickered with understanding, but he didn't

push. "Sure thing." Then he slipped past me and went into the house without another word.

My gaze returned to the tree line where Ryker's brown wolf was peeking at me from behind the tree trunks. He vanished, and bones cracked, informing me he was shifting back to human form. Moments later, he emerged in jeans, still pulling on a shirt as he walked toward me.

The way his abs rippled distracted me, and I noticed his wound had vanished from him being in animal form. Heat flooded my body, and my legs took a step toward him without my permission.

He frowned and stopped about fifteen feet from me, making it clear he didn't want to get any closer.

For some reason, I hadn't expected that, and I flinched outwardly. "I...I wanted to talk to you."

He laughed bitterly, making me realize that maybe he didn't want me at all anymore.

# CHAPTER TWENTY-ONE

"So *now* you want to talk?" His voice was sharp and harsh. "Right when we're getting ready to go fucking fight?"

My pulse quickened, and I forced myself to hold his gaze. "I wanted to talk to you the other night, but when Briar came into the room, you left."

He bared his teeth. "I stuck around after eating that steak, but you never joined me. In fact, you never came out of the bedroom."

The distance between us felt like a chasm, and my chest tightened. He had actually waited for me.

"I've been out here for three days, and right before we potentially have to find a witch, you decide it's time to talk?" He crossed his arms, his chest muscles taut beneath the fabric of his shirt. "If this is how you make yourself feel better before facing another threat, don't bother." He moved toward the door, passing right by me.

Snatching his arm, I turned him to face me, the jolt of the connection stronger than ever. My wolf surged forward, insistent I never let him go. "That's not fair." My voice cracked. "I didn't know you waited on me."

He pulled his arm out of my grip, his eyes a stormy haze. "That's what I do, Ember, ever since I realized I can't fight what I feel for you anymore. Wait on you. Chase you. But when it comes down to it, you're the one who keeps pushing me away. I bared my heart to you, and you told me you weren't ready. I respected that while holding out hope. Not anymore."

His words cut deep, and I struggled to find my voice. "I don't mean to push you away." My breathing was uneven. "I was confused. After everything that happened...after you didn't tell me about the magic...I didn't know if I could trust you."

For a moment, he just stood there, jaw clenched tight enough that I thought it might shatter. Then his expression gentled slightly. "You think this is all about me keeping secrets? You had one of your own."

He turned again, ready to end the conversation, but something in him hesitated long enough for me to close the gap between us.

"If I had told you that Raven talked to me about detecting magic on you, it would've meant you'd never be able to tell me yourself. I wanted you to confide in *me* and your pack. I kept hoping you would, but you never even seemed close to it."

"It's not something I'm proud of." He rubbed his jaw. "At first, I didn't care. I just didn't want the guys to know what I'd done because they'd worry. Finding whoever did this to my pack and our late royals was the priority. Nothing else mattered...until you came along. I should've known—you're a damn troublemaker." The corners of his lips tipped upward.

My heart skipped a beat. I tried to ignore the flutters because we had to work through these issues. "I wanted you to be open with me."

He lifted both hands. "Why? All it would do was give you another reason to push me away."

A knife pierced my heart. "That's not fair. My pack was slaughtered, my sister was missing, and all I wanted to do was find her and take her someplace safe. The last person I trusted killed everyone I loved."

He huffed. "Now I get what they say about the Sinclairs."

"What's that supposed to mean?" I stumbled back.

"That when things get complicated, you run. Royal blood or not, you aren't cut out to deal with anything messy. You hide and wait for the conflict to be over."

That hit a little too close to home. "Oh, so you get upset with me for believing rumors about you, but now you're using rumors against me."

His eyes flared. "They're not rumors if they're true, are they? You told me that was your plan. Get your sister and disappear."

Heat rose in my cheeks. "You asked me to leave! When I stayed, you were the one who told me to go."

"Of course I did!" His voice thundered in my ears. "I wanted you to be safe. That's the most important thing to me. I fucking lo–!" He winced, closing his mouth.

My heart lurched into my throat. Had he been about to say he loved me?

The words hung between us, and my head spun. His chest heaved with each breath, and he stood, vulnerable, in front of me.

"Do you have any idea how hard it is to see you fight your way in and out of my life?" He spoke softer now, but the words still had an edge that cut deep. "You're all I think about, Ember, even when I should be focused on keeping my pack alive. I fucking took a knife to save your sister because I couldn't bear the thought of you losing her."

A wave of conflicting emotions crashed over me. My wolf begged for me to close the distance between us again, but I was scared he'd reject me once more.

"I can't live without you either," I whispered.

His eyes widened, and his jaw clenched. "Then stop playing with me. Stop making me think I'm crazy for feeling this way and that it's one-sided."

I hated that he felt that way. My resolve broke, and I took a trembling breath. "I feel the same way about you, Ryker. It's definitely not one-sided."

Something unreadable crossed his face, and then he stalked forward, his attention focused on my lips.

Even though kissing him was the one thing I wanted to do, we hadn't truly resolved any of our problems. If he touched me, I'd forget that we still had an issue that would continue to fester.

I must have shied away because his expression fell, and he looked wounded all over again. He turned away and stepped around me to head inside.

"Please don't go," I rasped, clutching his arm. "It's not what you—"

"Tell me what you want from me, Ember." His voice was hoarse, cracking under the weight of everything unsaid. "I'll do whatever you want. I just need to know what that is. I can't keep doing this."

My throat tightened. "I want you to tell me the complete truth. I need to hear it all from you. I can't move forward unless we can both trust each other."

Our gazes locked, and the world stood still.

He released a long, shuddering sigh. "All right. I'll tell you everything."

The certainty in his voice sent a shiver down my spine. He reached for my hand, hesitating as if testing whether I would pull away again.

This time, I didn't. I was just as exhausted as him. I missed his touch... No, I *craved* it. I felt peace only when I touched or was close to him. I clasped his hand.

"After the attack on the royals, the only emotions I could feel were anger and pain. Some days, it was hard to function...to even get out of bed. Other days, my anger got the best of me. Nothing mattered except finding whoever did it, but I wasn't able to hold it together to actually make progress.

"One day, while we were eating in the kitchen here, Queen Ambrosia mentioned a witch nearby with the ability to manipulate the soul to help people focus on their end goals." His thumb rubbed against my wrist as he continued, "So, at the first opportunity, I went into the study and looked into it. I learned that a witch with that ability could cast a spell to take away my humanity." The words were raw, filled with something close to shame. "I asked Raven a question about the witch Ambrosia had mentioned, remarking that I knew witches usually tried to remain hidden. Raven made a comment about a possible location, and I was able to figure out where to find the witch. I found her, and she said she could cloak my soul so that I could focus on my end goal. All I had to do was give her some of my blood. I did."

He paused and examined my reaction.

I struggled to swallow, and I tried to school my expression, but my heart was breaking for him. I squeezed his hand tighter, wanting him to know I was on his side. "Is it still affecting you?"

"Yes, but it's getting weaker." He licked his lips. "And I think I know why."

His gaze burned into mine as I breathed, "Why?"

"Because you're my fated mate, Ember. That trumps everything, even this spell."

My heart stilled. I waited for disbelief to hit, but it didn't. Somehow, some way, Ryker being my fated mate made sense. But at the same time...it didn't. "Reid's rejection—"

"Doesn't matter. You're mine, Ember. I don't understand it either, but I'm so fucking glad you're the one made for me," he said fervently. "I should've realized it sooner. No matter what I do or how far you run, we're drawn back to each other."

The truth of his words resonated deep within me, and the walls I'd built to protect myself crumbled when they should've gotten stronger. But with Ryker, I wasn't scared. The fated-mate bond with Reid had never felt this secure.

He tucked a stray lock of hair behind my ear, his touch gentle despite the tension between us. "If we have each other, the rest doesn't matter."

All the strain left my body. "You're right. I'm sorry for not telling you when Raven informed me—"

He shook his head, cutting me off. "No, it's my fault. I should've confided in you when my feelings for you couldn't be ignored any longer. I should've been honest about what I'd done. I just was afraid you wouldn't look at me the same, and that thought petrified me."

"I'd never be able to look at you differently. Even though it doesn't make sense to me, I do believe you're my other half, and I'm tired of fighting it."

He smiled and leaned down to kiss me, but I placed a hand on his chest, holding him back.

He grimaced, so I quickly said, "I want to kiss you. I do." Hell, I wanted to do a lot more than that with him. I was finally done fighting what was brewing between us. These last three days had been pure hell. "But first, is there anything else you've hidden from me?"

"Nothing." His gaze held mine with unwavering intensity, and the lack of sulfur confirmed he wasn't lying. "What about you?"

My mouth dried. This was it. However, I didn't want to make him more of a target than he already was. "I've told you everything, but Ryker, there's something wrong with me. It might be for the best if you still keep your distance. I mean, I can see the enemy, and Reid said at the—"

"Dammit, Ember. There is *nothing* wrong with you. Can't you see that Reid only said that to make you look weak so his pack could try to take control?" His nostrils flared. "I'll make him pay for what he did to you—for all we know, his witch cast some spell on you to make you see these things, so you'll believe you're losing your mind." His irises glowed as his own wolf peeked through. "I'm not fucking going anywhere. Do you understand?"

Even though my head screamed *don't*, my heart and soul believed him. At barely a whisper, I said, "I do."

Relief washed over his features as he drew me closer with a raw urgency that ignited every cell in my body. He rasped, "No more secrets." Our chests pressed together, and his warm, minty breath hit my lips. "I really need to kiss you right now."

This time, I didn't hold back. My mouth met his fiercely, and the world disappeared. Only the two of us existed.

Heat coursed through me as his hands tangled in my hair and pulled me closer, erasing any distance between us. His lips moved against mine with a ferocity that should've scared me, but it only fueled my own.

I kissed him back hard, my fingers digging into his arms like he might disappear if I didn't hold on tight enough. Even if I wanted to stop, I couldn't. Electricity shot between us, and a knot of need twisted deep inside me.

The bond roared to life, powerful and undeniable. My wolf howled in triumph, urging me to claim him and let nothing stand in the way of what we were meant to be. He backed me toward the trees, and within seconds, my shoulders hit rough bark while his body pressed against mine.

He rained kisses down my face until his lips pressed against the base of my neck. His teeth grazed the artery where I craved for him to bite me. "We should stop," he groaned as his hands slid underneath the hem of my shirt.

He couldn't be serious. That was the last thing I wanted to do. I needed him to fill me...to claim me...to mix his scent with mine. Yet, if he wasn't ready, it wasn't fair for me to push him. "Do you want to?" Still, my hands eased under his shirt, and my nails dug into his back.

He shuddered, making me feel so damn powerful.

"Ember, you deserve better than forming the bond outside the vampire mansion when we're both drunk with lust." His teeth dug a little bit deeper into my neck despite his protests. "We should be alone, with no chance of anyone interrupting us."

If that was what he was worried about, then it wasn't an issue. I didn't think my wolf would allow me to wait another minute. I freed my left hand and pressed his face harder against my neck, ready to feel the sting of his teeth inside me.

He growled, catching my hand and pulling it down to my side. His tongue caressed where he'd drawn a little blood, and heat seared through me. His other hand moved under my bra, cupping my breast. "It's your turn to be patient," he murmured, his voice rough with desire.

A shiver of pleasure raced through me even as I moaned in protest. His thumb brushed over my nipple, and my breath caught. I grew dizzy. This man knew exactly how to unravel me.

"Patient?" At this point, I wasn't above begging. "I've been patient for way too long."

His chest rumbled against mine in a satisfied laugh before he kissed me again, and his other hand slid underneath the waist of my sweatpants. His fingers immediately slid between my folds and found the right spot.

No one had ever known my body so well before, and this was his first time touching me this way.

"When we complete the bond, I want it to be perfect."

He circled faster and harder, already building tension inside me. I followed his lead, sliding my hands under his waistband and grabbing him.

Ryker groaned into my neck, his hips bucking as I stroked him in time with his fingers. His muscles responded beneath my touch, and I longed for more. I tugged at his jeans, needing him free so he could get inside me.

"Fuck," he gasped, pressing me harder against the tree. I could feel how close he was to losing control, and it thrilled me.

I tried to spin him so he was against the tree and I could take charge, but he caught my arm.

"No." He pressed harder against me and growled, "Not like this. Not when another man could come out here and see you naked."

I quivered at his possessiveness, and excitement shot through me.

"You don't seem to mind someone watching you pleasure me while my clothes are on, though," I teased as I quickened my pace.

His fingers worked me faster, and I lost all sense of anything except how damn good his hand felt. "That's different." His eyes burned into mine, and my wolf bayed at the raw desire written across his features.

My body coiled tight as I got closer and closer to release. He swallowed hard as I moved my hand over him, building the same tension inside him. "Ember..." He groaned my name like a warning just before I shattered beneath his touch.

My body shook as his name ripped from my throat. My legs went weak, but the tree and Ryker's body kept me upright.

I gripped him tighter, knowing I had to finish him, demanding he come at the same time. My own ecstasy strengthened. His muscles strained, and he buried his face against my shoulder as he grunted with his own release.

Our hands stilled, our breaths coming out in ragged gasps, but everything had already begun building inside me again. This wasn't enough. He had to be *in* me.

"I saw fucking stars, lil rebel." He chuckled, peppering kisses all along my face.

"Imagine what it'll feel like when we complete our bond." I leaned back and kissed him once more, enjoying the way our tongues collided.

But then Briar linked, *Ember, we've got to go. Something went wrong.*

# CHAPTER TWENTY-TWO

I stiffened against him, the urgency of Briar's message slicing through the haze of desire. Reality flooded back in a rush, reminding me why I'd held myself back from Ryker and this connection in the first place.

"What is it?" Ryker pulled away slightly, brows furrowed.

"Briar." Dread settled heavily in my bones. "Something's up."

"Of course my pack wouldn't alert me." His jaw clenched, and he exhaled a shaky breath. "The witch?"

I nodded, forcing myself not to step forward and close the small gap between us. My wolf whimpered, and an emptiness ached deep inside my heart. "She's essential if we're going to stop these attacks. We should go inside."

He kissed me once more as though sealing a promise, then pulled back with obvious reluctance. "Let's go."

We fixed our clothes in silence, both of us battling the bond that screamed at us to stay together. He took my hand, sending sparks through my body and giving me comfort that we were in this together.

*Ember, this isn't a joke,* Briar connected again, her frustration surging through the connection. *The Shae pack's backup are close by and want us to meet them. The witch returned a lot quicker than any of us expected.*

"We won't have a bond for long if we can't stop the Blackwoods." I didn't hide the fear in my voice. *We're on our way.*

Ryker's hand tightened. "They'll make a mistake. Maybe if we can capture the witch, we can get some answers."

He tugged me toward the back door, and my wolf eased forward. The yank to complete the bond ebbed with a goal in sight. Not only did we all want to save our species and protect our own kind, but now I had an added incentive to be able to complete the bond with Ryker and live a long life by his side.

We rushed inside to find Kendric, Gage, Xander, Briar, and Raven standing in the center of the living room. No other vampire was there, which was the norm since we'd begun staying here.

Kendric stood, his posture unyielding. He and Raven were about ten feet apart, silent and stiff, proving that their spat wasn't over. Xander and Gage exchanged a glance, and their frowns deepened at the sight of Ryker. Even in a crisis, they weren't going to make it easy on him. Briar paced the center of the room with restless energy.

"What's going on?" Ryker demanded.

Gage gave a humorless chuckle. "Oh, now you'll join us. It's nice to see you again, *alpha.*"

Ryker's expression darkened, and his entire body went rigid.

"The witch came back thirty minutes after she left." Briar tugged at the ends of her hair. "The Shae pack backup is about twenty-five minutes away, which means we ought to get moving to scout the area."

Okay. This wasn't nearly as awful as Briar had made it sound, but even now, anxiety wafted from her.

For her to be this upset, I had to be missing something. Instead of focusing on her worry, we needed to discuss facts. That should help her process what came next. "Is it Cassi? The pack witch?"

Raven shrugged. "Unclear. The ones watching aren't sure what the witch looks like."

A chill swept through me. "The Blackwoods were keeping her hidden." I'd never realized it before now. "The first time I saw her was the day the fated-mate bond flared between Reid and me. And then I saw her a second time at the ceremony." I tried to word the last part carefully, not wanting to reiterate the fact that I'd come close to mating with another person.

Ryker's body vibrated, making it clear that he understood exactly which ceremony I was referring to. "I'll take great pleasure in killing the asshole."

"I'm pretty sure that's the real Ryker talking, but who fucking knows anymore." Gage wrinkled his nose and crossed his arms.

Xander lifted a brow. "Ember should know. Does he have signs of the magic influencing him right now?"

My stomach churned. I did *not* want to become a pawn in Ryker's pack issues. We hadn't completed the bond, and we were still two separate packs.

Ryker's eyes flashed with anger, and a familiar darkness settled over him. "We don't have time for this."

The sheen still hadn't appeared, but I didn't want to say that because I feared it would make the situation worse.

"Listen, don't put me in the middle of your pack arguments."

Gage snorted. "Please. You've been upset with him over the same thing. Just because you two clearly made up doesn't mean that we've decided to forgive him."

The uneasiness in the room spiked, an awkward silence hanging around us.

We didn't have time for this nonsense. "We're wasting time fighting each other when we need to be focused on the real enemy—the Blackwoods. Or did you all forget about them and how they've killed the majority of our packs and families?"

The men glanced down at the wooden floors, refusing to look me in the eye.

Good.

I looked at Briar. "You said the Shae pack is close?"

Briar slowed her pacing while Raven placed a hand on her stomach and answered, "Yes. Bruce called, asking for you, but you weren't here, so he agreed to talk with me instead."

My breath caught. I didn't understand why, but I didn't like him talking to Raven. Even though I trusted her, and the vampires were clearly our allies—Queen Ambrosia had even punished her son on live video for other vampires to see what would happen if they turned humans into vampires—Ryker and I were the middlemen between our two species.

Teeth grinding like he felt similarly to me, Ryker asked, "What did he say?"

Wringing her hands, Raven sat in the center of the leather couch and looked at each of us except for Kendric. She repeated what Briar had already told me but added a little more. "He has about forty pack members spread throughout the Sinclair property and the property line from the Blackwoods' territory to the national park. The witch they located is on the national park side, so everyone but ten moved in that direction. They're trying to make sure their scent doesn't get detected so the Blackwoods won't know they're being watched."

So we still had the element of surprise. That had to count for something. "But they have no idea which witch it is or who picked her up to take her wherever?"

"Bruce mentioned it was someone from the Blackwood pack."

"We need someone who's seen Cassi to go there." Ryker shook his head.

As if Ryker hadn't just spoken, Gage focused his attention on me. "What do you want to do, Ember?"

I froze, understanding exactly what they were doing. And I didn't appreciate it at *all*.

Kendric nodded. "It's your call."

I bit back my frustration. Ryker's pack didn't respect him, and I had a feeling this was their way of testing his authority. He was still their alpha, even if they didn't agree with how he'd handled things, and if I gave in and answered, it would only make matters worse, both between them and between Ryker and me.

Ryker put his hand on my shoulder and squeezed—a silent thank-you for letting him handle this, and said, "We take two vehicles, so if one of the packs calls for backup, some of us can split off. Xander, Kendric, and Gage in one car. Briar, Ember, Raven, and myself in another."

"I get why splitting up sounds ideal, but I think we're stronger if we stay together." Raven tapped on her phone. "Queen Ambrosia's offered to let us take one of our Suburbans so we can all fit in one car. We can head out now, and

Lucinda and the other guards will come as backup closer to the time we decide to move in case it gets ugly, so there isn't a real benefit to us dividing."

Raven's fingers stopped moving. "She wants to know if there's anything else we require that she can provide." Her eyes flicked up to where Kendric stood.

I sucked in a breath. Once again, the queen was being super helpful to the shifters. All the rumors of distrust and hatred were being refuted, and I wondered if the Black-woods had been behind them all with an end goal in sight. After all, who would've suspected they would go so far as to kill the entire royal family and their guards?

"If Ambrosia is offering, let's take her up on it." Ryker dropped his hands to his sides. "I know we've been staying in human form to communicate with the vampires and with Ember and Briar. But we should all change into clothes that are easy to take on and off in case we have to shift. We aren't sure what we're walking into."

Kendric, Xander, and Gage stood still, refusing to budge.

I linked to Briar, *Please do as Ryker requested. We need to get moving, and I need to talk to these three idiots alone.*

*Fine with me.* My sister nodded and headed into the bedroom. *I'll grab our clothes so we can change in the bathroom and the guys can have the room.*

*Thank you.*

Ryker growled, and Raven watched the mutiny unfolding before her. I hated that the very people she was trying to help were acting like a bunch of children.

"I said go change. We don't have time for this bullshit." His eyes glowed, the wolf coming forward.

"What?" Gage lifted his chin in defiance. "You gonna alpha-will us again? Now at least I know why you didn't have a fucking problem with it before. We cut you slack because we thought your behavior was due to the loss of our pack. But no. You had your humanity turned off, even around us."

This was going nowhere. I turned to Ryker, hoping he didn't get angry at my request. "Do you mind if I talk to them alone for a minute?" Briar headed out of the room with two sets of black shirts and sweatpants.

His eyes narrowed, but as he stared into mine, some of the tension flowed from his body, and his shoulders relaxed ever so slightly. "Fine."

He brushed a hand along my arm, the sparks springing to life. This had to be his way of telling me that he wasn't mad at me.

Silence filled the room as Ryker left. He glanced back at me one last time before shutting the door behind him.

When I turned to the three of them, I noticed Raven and Kendric staring at one another.

I felt like an ass for doing this, but Raven wasn't a wolf shifter and didn't understand pack relationships. I didn't want her influencing the others because of her lack of understanding. "Do you want us to meet you out front when we're ready?"

Her attention jerked to me. She tilted her head, and her face tightened for a moment. "Sure. That sounds great. I'll be outside in five minutes." She left too.

As soon as her footsteps faded, I jumped to the point. "Look. What Ryker did is shitty, but this is not the time to fight each other. The Blackwoods are working with a witch, probably more than one, which means things are going to get deadlier—and fast."

Xander rubbed the back of his neck. "You trust him after what happened? Just like that?"

"Yes, I trust him. But I understand if you're not ready yet." I laced my fingers together. "No matter what, Ryker is your alpha. I'll talk with him and ask him to tell you all if the magic impacts him again. If he doesn't, I'll know because I can see when it's working on him."

Xander and Gage exchanged glances, and Kendric folded his arms. All their eyes glowed, informing me they were communicating through their pack links. I wanted to hurry the conversation, but at least they were discussing how to move forward.

"We need to work together until we get through this mess," I added, hoping to quicken their decision. "I believe Ryker has learned a hard lesson, especially given how important you three are to him."

The lines on Kendric's face softened, but his expression remained skeptical. "I'm so sick and tired of not being told critical information and not being part of decisions. I understand that I might not like what's decided, but I would at least like to have my voice heard. After the three of you pulled that shit the other day, and then we learned about Ryker being spelled, I don't know who I can trust anymore."

"I'm sorry." I hung my head. Excluding them hadn't been done on purpose, but we shouldn't have left them in the dark. I'd even treated Briar that way, and at the end of the day, when you hurt someone, your intentions didn't matter. The damage was done. "I regret not informing Briar."

"You'll make sure that, if you tell her something, she'll tell us too?" Xander placed a hand on his hip.

They still didn't trust Ryker, but they trusted me and were willing to play nice with him. "I promise." Going forward, I'd need to tell Ryker what I was informing Briar of so he had the chance to tell his pack before she did. Trust was easy to lose and hard to build back up.

Gage let out a breath that sounded like surrender while Kendric lifted both hands and said, "Okay. But we're counting on you, Ember."

That wasn't exactly what I wanted, but I'd take it for now. "Thank you. Now let's get ready. We're meeting Raven outside in a few minutes."

The three of them headed off to the bedroom, and I walked down the hall to the bathroom Briar was in. I knocked on the door and linked, *It's me.*

The door cracked open, and I entered, finding her already dressed. I quickly removed my clothing and sneakers then grabbed the black shirt and put it on.

*What was all that about?* She leaned against the sink, watching me.

Snagging the sweatpants, I pulled them on too. *We can't have them refusing to listen to Ryker at all, so I needed to talk to them. They're going to put aside their issues for now, but they're still skeptical.*

Briar gathered her hair into a ponytail. *What's with the sudden change between you and him?*

*We talked and addressed everything with each other.* I followed suit, twisting my hair into a bun and slipping my sneakers back on. *It's a long story, and I do trust him now, but if he ruins my trust again, there won't be any salvaging what we have.*

She smiled and kissed my cheek. *I firmly believe that when he realized how much he loved you, he didn't know how to tell you because he'd kept it from everyone for so long. He won't make that mistake with you again.*

He loved me.

I could've sworn that was what he'd been about to say

earlier before he stopped himself. My heart skipped a beat, and I exhaled noisily. I couldn't get all emotional and lovey-dovey now. Not when there was so much at stake. This would have to wait. *Let's go.*

The two of us walked out to find the four guys waiting for us at the end of the hallway. I nodded at Ryker, and he somehow understood and led us through the living room and out the front door. The Suburban waited for us with Raven in the driver's seat.

Instead of Kendric, Gage climbed into the front passenger seat, which spoke volumes. Raven scowled as Xander, Kendric, and Briar got into the back row, Briar smack in the middle. Ryker and I took the middle row, with me sitting behind Raven.

As soon as we were all settled, she pulled out of the circle and headed toward our destination. Silence filled the vehicle as we sped down the winding mountain trail toward Blackwood territory. The air buzzed with stress, but we all knew this temporary truce was necessary if we wanted to make it through alive.

As we passed the narrow dirt road that led to our pack lands, Briar's anxiety vibrated through our pack link. I glanced over my shoulder to see her glance down the road with glistening eyes.

Of course...that was why she'd been upset earlier. She'd realized we'd have to pass by our lands in order to get to the Blackwoods' and might relive memories and the attack once again. I couldn't offer her comforting words because nothing could fix the grief. The missing pack links of all our members were still ice cold in my chest, reminding me of what we'd lost. So, I did the only thing I could do. *We'll get justice for them.*

When her unease receded and her resolve seeped into

our connection, she replied, *That's what I hope for, Ember. Justice, not vengeance. I need the Blackwoods to realize that what they did isn't okay. That each individual life should matter.*

*Then that's what we'll do. We'll make sure they remember them.*

No more words were necessary, both of us focusing on the promise we'd just made. Soon we were driving through the woods past the Blackwood property line, heading to the area next to theirs, Shadowbrook National Park.

Once we pulled off the highway and maneuvered through gravel roads and thick woods, Raven took an abrupt turn that led to a little-used parking area.

Bruce was leaning against his huge pickup truck, talking to three men. As soon as Raven pulled in behind him and parked, he headed to our vehicle.

He came to my door and opened it while pointing deeper into the oak forest that would lead us to the edge of the national park and the Blackwoods' territory. "Just through those trees. We'll take a short hike in so the cars won't be seen." His gaze traveled over all of us, lingering on Ryker with a calculating look before focusing back on me. "Are all of you ready?"

Even Bruce didn't fully trust Ryker. "We're ready," I said, climbing out of the car.

"Good. Let's move and see what we can figure out." Bruce nodded once, his eyes glowing as the other three men moved deeper into the woods and waited for us.

Ryker tensed beside me, but he stayed silent as we exited and joined Bruce alongside the vehicles.

Raven moved to my other side, and we followed Bruce and his three men deeper into the woods, with Briar,

Xander, Kendric, and Gage taking up the rear. I tapped into my wolf hearing, finding nothing out of the norm.

We continued on, but then I did notice something telling—there weren't any animal noises. The realization made my skin crawl, and I grabbed Ryker's wrist. He glanced at me and squinted, but I couldn't risk talking. Not now. What if we were being watched?

Bruce stopped dead in his tracks and spun around, his eyes glowing brightly. "The Blackwoods just discovered my packmates."

# CHAPTER TWENTY-THREE

The panic in Bruce's eyes and voice told us everything. "They're demanding that the eleven of us come there. They want to know what we're doing out here."

I growled. They fucking knew why we were here. They'd attacked all three of our packs. Did they expect us to just lie down and wait for them to finish us off? I'd rather die fighting than lay myself out for slaughter.

"How could they have snuck up on them?" Raven placed a hand on her chest. "Your pack would've heard them approach."

Ryker laughed bitterly. "Not when they're able to cloak themselves. If this doesn't prove they're behind all of this, I don't know what will."

"All I know is that they have twenty of my pack surrounded, which is damn near half of what they left alive. We have to listen to them." Bruce fisted his hands. "I can't lose any more people."

Ryker's jaw tightened. "Ember and Briar don't have to be there. This could be a setup. The women can go back to the Suburban and leave while my pack goes with you to handle this."

For a moment, all I could do was blink. I must have heard him wrong. There was no *way* he expected me to leave instead of remaining by his side.

Frustration lined Bruce's face. "It's not that simple. My pack said they know exactly who's here." His voice rose, edged with desperation. "They demanded all of us."

The sun was setting, causing the shadows of the trees to lengthen. Almost like the shadows the Blackwoods used to cloak themselves were laughing at us.

*We have to help them, Ember,* Briar linked, her determination filtering through me. *We can't leave them behind. I'm not sure if I'll ever get over what Dad forced us to do that night.*

That would haunt me for the rest of my life as well. Though I doubted we'd have survived if he hadn't, what if we had? Maybe I could've seen the shadows that night too, but I'd been forced to run before I was given the opportunity. "There's no way Briar and I are leaving. Both of us will go with you."

Raven's phone dinged, and she swiped the screen. "Lucinda just texted. They're loading the weapons now and will be on their way shortly. If things go bad, they should arrive in time to help."

"Then that's even more of a reason not to disagree. If the Blackwoods want us there," I said, my voice firm with newfound resolve, "then we're going. All of us."

Ryker snarled, and his eyes glowed with barely contained frustration. His wolf surged forward, wanting to command me but knowing at the same time it wouldn't work. I wasn't part of his pack...not yet.

Gage sidled between Ryker and me, and Ryker flushed.

Gage stood firm and crossed his arms. "We're not going unless she's with us. And if you try to force us, I will join her pack and leave your ass behind."

Between those words and the way Ryker glowered, my heart cracked in my chest. I never wanted to come between him and his pack, and I definitely didn't want people leaving him to join me.

Xander nodded. "It'll cause even more problems if we all split up."

"We don't have time for this." Bruce kicked at the mulchy ground. "I can't risk something else happening to my pack."

I took Ryker's hand, afraid that he would drop it. When he didn't, I tugged on it as the jolts shot between us. "Let's go."

His shoulders sagged, but he nodded.

We hurried through the forest, the trees thickening as we closed in on the invisible line that separated the park from the Blackwood territory.

Each crunch of leaves underfoot seemed amplified in the ominous silence, as if emphasizing that we were entering a very ambiguous situation.

A small clearing opened up, and I could see people clustered together about fifty yards from the edge of the territory.

As we got closer, I managed to pick out Perry and Reid standing in the center of Bruce's people with at least fifty of their pack members circling them. There was no telling how many more were hiding in the woods and cloaked in darkness.

In my periphery, I searched for signs of iridescent shadows blending in with the darkening sky.

Perry and Reid stepped forward, the alpha and beta of

the pack as well as father and son. They almost appeared to be carbon copies of each other, Perry the older version.

Reid's sparkling blue eyes locked with mine then lowered to Ryker's and my joined hands. The corner of his lips tugged downward. "I hate that you got caught up in this mess."

Striding in front of me, Ryker moved so Reid couldn't see me. He gritted, "You don't get to talk to her. You talk to me instead."

No.

He didn't get to take away my chance for at least partial answers. I moved around him, catching Ryker by surprise. Within seconds, his widened eyes narrowed, and I saw when he accepted that, once again, I wasn't going to listen to him.

"If you didn't want me caught up in this *mess*, Reid, maybe you shouldn't have murdered my pack." I was done tiptoeing around them. It was time for the gloves to come off.

"And we're all here as requested." Bruce's hands shook like his shift was coming on. "So let my people go. You've killed enough of them."

The wind blew, lifting Reid's shaggy blond hair. "Murdered your..." He looked dumbfounded. "Killed your pack members?" His voice went alarmingly high, a sound that I hoped he wouldn't be able to reproduce.

"What is she talking about?" Perry ran a hand through his short, dark-blond hair. "Did you do something to the Sinclair and Shae packs?"

"Of course not." Reid straightened to his full six-foot-three-inch frame. "I don't know what they mean."

Ryker pointed at him. "Don't lie to us. We all know

what you've done. You set *us* up to take the fall so you can lead everyone."

Jaw dropping, Reid stared at me and said, "I get that I embarrassed you at the ceremony. I don't know what came over me, but I swear I never meant to act that way or hurt you. But you can't believe our pack to be so evil as to..." He squared his shoulders. "*He* got you to believe that. And you'd know if I were lying." His gaze shifted from me. "And Bruce, our packs have been friends with yours for decades. We'd never harm you."

"Unless your scent was cloaked, Reid." Raven's voice cut through the strain, reminding us all of the power they had on their side.

"Cloaked?" Reid's brows furrowed, and he exchanged puzzled looks with Perry and the rest of the Blackwood pack. Their expressions were so genuinely confused that I almost believed them.

A chill snaked down my spine, and cold pressure closed in from all sides.

A lump lodged in my throat, and my entire body tensed.

Reid turned toward me, his entire attention on me. "What's wrong?"

"They're coming." The pressure increased, and it felt as if a tsunami were barreling toward me to pull me under.

Perry whipped his head toward me. "Who's coming? And why the hell is the Shae pack spying on us?"

"Maybe..." Gage drew out the word. "They're curious what backstabbing bastards look like."

The pressure strengthened further, suffocating and thick. I scanned the area, my heart racing as wisps of shadows emerged slowly from the trees. They coiled closer, surrounding the Blackwood pack with eerie precision.

"The shadows are surrounding them. They have to be controlling them." I wanted to ask Raven how close the vampires were, but I didn't want the Blackwoods to know that we had backup on the way. At this point, the vampires should be arriving any second.

"Shadows?" A tall woman from the Blackwood pack spun around. "What is she talking about?" Her voice cracked with fear.

That...didn't make sense.

"Don't worry. The vampires will arrive in two minutes." Raven told them the exact information I didn't want anyone beyond our group to know.

Why would she tell them that?

*What do you need me to do?* Briar linked as her fear took hold.

I wasn't sure how to answer, so I said the only thing I could think of at the moment. *Survive.*

Slowly, I spun around. We were completely surrounded.

"We should run," a red-haired man from the Shae pack said. "Don't wait for them to attack."

This wasn't supposed to happen. "We're already surrounded."

"What are you—" an older man from the Shae pack started to ask, but then a shadow reached for his neck and shredded his throat.

More shadows poured from the trees with terrifying, coordinated speed. Before anyone could react, they swarmed the Shae pack and us, dark forms tearing into our lines. Screams of pain and surprise pierced the air, and blood sprayed across the clearing.

The Blackwoods weren't the target. They were never

going to be. They'd just bought time to get their fighters set up, and we'd fallen for it.

I spun around and saw a shadow at Ryker's back.

"Ryker, behind you!" I shouted just as the shadow lunged with its arms extended.

He ducked, and the arm caught only air.

Briar's panic coursed through me like it had a life of its own. I turned to find three shadows converging on her.

I had to help her. Hell, I had to help everyone!

The Blackwood pack wasn't being harmed, but several screamed and ran from the clearing. Shadows broke away, chasing them, possibly intending for them to never make it home.

Chaos ensued, and I could only watch as the slaughter commenced.

The shadows ripped through the clearing like a storm, relentless and merciless. They played with us, injuring and drawing out each attack with cruel precision. A dark mass ripped through the red-haired man's side, his yell echoing in my mind before he collapsed.

Panic spread as quickly as the blood on the ground. I wasn't sure what to do, and I couldn't help but notice that none of them were attacking me.

Briar's scream cut through the chaos, high and wild. I spun around to find a shadow wrapped around her small frame, its claws sinking deep into her sides.

Another one pounced on Ryker, clawing his leg. Ryker fought, trying to grab the shadow, and managed to hold him off, but not for long. All the others were in the same predicament.

If I wanted as many people as possible to live, I had to make the shadows focus on me.

I glanced around and saw a gun in a dying Shae pack member's waistband.

I ran over and yanked it from the holster, its weight awkward and foreign as I gripped it. My grandfather had taught me to shoot in case we ever got dragged into violence, but it had been more than a decade since I'd held a gun. As soon as my father became alpha, shooting lessons were one of the first things he told me I didn't need.

If only Dad were alive to see that Grandfather had been right to teach me....

Tightening my chest against that pain, I tried to recall what I'd been shown and aimed at the shadow crushing Briar. My hands shook, and with a deep breath, I pulled the trigger, praying to Fate that I hit my mark and not her.

The bang split through the chaos like lightning, and the shot didn't hit center mass as I'd aimed for, but the lower part of the shadow's body. It loosened its grip on Briar with a yelp, giving her a moment to gasp for air and wriggle free.

The shadows halted mid-attack, all of them turning toward me. Though they had no eyes, I felt their gazes prickling over my skin like icy needles.

I fired again, wanting them to attack me. The bullet hit a shadow closing in on Ryker. Its grip faltered, giving him the chance to push free with a savage kick.

My wolf came to the fore, ready to shift.

"Get your guns and fire as they attack you!" I bellowed, half animal and human. "That's the only way we're going to live through this."

Almost in tandem, the shadows charged at me. I spun around, yanking my clothes off as my wolf broke free. My bones cracked, but I kept moving, knowing I needed to gain distance from them, or I was as good as dead.

My back broke, and I was running on my hands and feet until they turned into paws underneath me.

A shadow swiped my side, and I whimpered as I took off toward Blackwood territory. We'd come here to find the witch, and I would try like hell to reach her.

I didn't pause when Ryker yelled my name. The wound ached, but I pushed through and kept going.

The shadows managed to keep up with me as I raced through the trees. My breath came in ragged bursts, and they closed in, swift and unrelenting. One lunged from my right, tearing into my shoulder and sending a searing pain across my upper body.

I stumbled but forced myself onward, knowing I had to keep moving or it would be over. Another shadow swiped at my hind leg. My muscles screamed with every step, frantic and despairing, but I kept running.

Glancing over my shoulder, I noticed that a huge number were chasing me. At least that would give the others a better chance to survive.

Blackwood territory wasn't far—if I could make it there, maybe I could find and kill the witch behind all this and end the terror.

A dark form bolted ahead of me, cutting off my escape route. I tried to change course, but more gathered in my path, uniting to block my way. I halted, sharp agony from my injuries ripping through me.

Shadows swarmed from every direction, closing the gaps and multiplying before my eyes. I was surrounded. Trapped.

A claw sliced across my side, and I yelped and fell to the ground.

A massive shadow loomed over me, menacing and deliberate, as if contemplating its next move. Its hand extended slowly, letting me know I was about to die.

Out of nowhere, a searing warmth burst between the shadow and me, and I had no doubt that I'd soon be heading toward the light.

# CHAPTER TWENTY-FOUR

The warmth dissipated as quickly as it had come. The shadows closed in, unfazed by whatever magic had hit us. If the shadows weren't worried about it, then maybe this magic would make my death more tragic and painful than I had initially realized.

The dark limb reaching for me lowered toward my chest, making its target clear. I braced and flipped to my stomach, pain from my injuries exploding down my side and legs.

I lifted my head, preparing to attack, and the shadow struck. I bared my teeth just as its hand seemed to collide with a solid wall. The impact sent a shock wave through the air, leaving a ripple where there should have been nothing.

An invisible barrier? That shouldn't have been possible, but the magic that surrounded me was now caressing my skin. The strange new presence inside me vibrated as if in tune.

The shadow recoiled and hesitated before striking again.

I flinched, hackles rising, but the shadow merely

collided with the invisible barrier again, causing an even bigger ripple.

Realization hit me: This was similar to the shield that had saved me during the attack on the Shae pack territory when we were freeing Briar. Whatever magic had guarded me then was protecting me now.

But how was that possible?

A chill bled in from behind me, and I spun around and found another shadow right on me. I steeled myself, muscles coiled for pain that didn't come. Instead, another resounding shock wave echoed around me, and another shadow reeled back, unable to touch me.

I had no time to investigate the barrier. Most of the shadows that had followed me were going back, and I needed to rejoin the others. Gunshots continued to fire from that direction, and there was no telling what was happening. I headed forward, right into several shadows that tried to block me, but as I stepped toward them, the barrier pushed them away from me. The ripples were disorienting, but I had a mission that I refused to fail—getting back to Ryker, Briar, and the others. I had to protect them from the Blackwoods, and this barrier around me would help me do it—if it lasted.

Shadows lunged again and again, assaulting the barrier with relentless force, but no matter what, they couldn't get to me. In fact, I couldn't even feel them ramming into the barrier.

Despite the agony from my wounds, I increased my speed, needing to help the people that I loved—in fact, the only people I truly had left.

The gunshots stopped, which had my chest clenching tight. *Briar, please tell me you're okay.*

*Believe it or not, we are. Are you? Hurry back.* Her dread

wafted through the bond, adding to the huge knot forming in my gut. *I wanted to reach out to you but was afraid I'd distract you. The witch is here with us.*

The witch.

I opened my mouth, my tongue rolling out as I took in deep, gasping breaths. I pushed myself to get there faster. *I'm coming. Don't worry.*

*It's the Blackwood witch, Cassi. She's confused by the magic she's sensing here, but the shadows have retreated.*

I glanced behind me, and my legs slowed of their own accord. All the shadows had vanished. This had to be a trick.

"I'm telling you, the Blackwoods would never work with a witch who uses this sort of magic." Cassi's voice was a little high with surprise or panic but still strong. "If they did, I wouldn't be here with them. That would cross the line of what I'm comfortable with."

"She could be lying," Raven said quickly. "We shouldn't trust her."

"I hate to say this, but Perry is dead, and Reid is near death." Ryker sighed. "The Blackwoods being behind this attack doesn't make sense."

Ryker.

My pulse pounded.

When I burst into the clearing, Reid's pale form was the first thing I saw. His neck had a deep wound, and blood soaked his gray shirt. Cassi was leaning over him, applying some sort of ointment with practiced efficiency and pressing a cloth to his neck.

With him being in that state, where in the world was his mate?

My stomach churned when I noted Perry about twenty

feet away on the ground, his throat ripped out and his chest still.

Several other pack members littered the ground. However, my gaze landed on the two most important people in the world—Ryker and Briar.

Briar sat on a log, blood oozing from wounds on her arms. Her face was drawn, but her eyes locked onto mine. Ryker stood beside her with his arms crossed despite the injury on his shoulder where a shadow's claws had cut through the material of his shirt.

Raven paced at the edge of the clearing with her phone in hand, her fingers hurriedly typing, while Kendric, Xander, and Gage, not being able to see the shadows, held guns and continued to scan the area on high alert.

I couldn't believe it, but every single shadow was gone. They'd retreated this way and kept going? *Right now, we're in the clear.*

Briar relayed the information to everyone.

Immediately, Ryker's eyes met mine, and he hurried to me.

Cassi's back straightened, and she jerked her head in my direction. "Wait. You're telling me that Ember can *see* the cloaked people?" Her shock and discomfort were too real for her to be faking. "I can't believe it," she muttered. "That's not possible...unless—"

"Unless what?" Ryker stood next to me, scanning my injuries. His fingers threaded into my fur, causing my body to heat despite the dire situation.

Cassi's gaze never left me. She answered, "Unless something more powerful is at work. Something that shouldn't be possible. But I can't ignore what's going on here."

Ryker looked around. "Perry's dead. Reid was nearly killed. I think we've been wrong about the Blackwoods. I don't know if we can trust Cassi, but if what she said about the shadows is true, this isn't making sense."

"She's messing with us." Raven stopped typing and wrinkled her nose. "This whole time, you've believed it's the Blackwoods, and just like that, you're willing to forget all the evidence we've seen up until now because of a *witch*?"

The wind stirred, leaves rustling across the forest floor. In the darkening sky, I almost didn't notice the iridescent shadow on the ground at the edge of the clearing until some leaves got stuck on its body.

I blinked, making sure my mind wasn't playing tricks on me. *Briar, there's an unmoving shadow over there.* I nodded my head toward it.

Overriding my impulse to stay next to Ryker, I trotted to the body. I glanced around, wondering if there were more, but saw no sign of any others. The shadows must have carried their dead away, but they hadn't been able to retrieve this one from behind the strange protective barrier.

Gage moved over to me and lifted a brow. "What's going on?"

I linked with Briar. *Tell them what I'm seeing.* She informed the others.

Ryker, Briar, Gage, Xander, and Kendric ran to my side as Cassi's head jerked toward the five members of the Black-wood pack who were still in the clearing. She said, "One of you take over here and keep pressure on his wound. If you don't, he'll die."

A woman who was probably in her thirties rushed over and placed her hands on Reid's wound. Cassi stood and marched to me.

"We should leave it alone," Raven said in a tight voice. "It could be a trap."

"Not possible." Cassi held out her hands over the shadow. "I'm using magic to make sure the shadows are repelled and won't return. Whoever is responsible for these attacks clearly didn't anticipate the presence of my spells." Her gaze was calculating as she took in the empty air around us. "I can feel the vile magic that Ember detected."

Ryker's jaw clenched. "Can you uncloak it?"

"I can try." Cassi kneeled beside me. She reached out a hand and lowered it over the shadow.

"Holy shit," Xander muttered. "It's like her hand is resting on air."

"This is a bad idea. This witch doesn't have cloaking magic. None of us should mess with it." Raven appeared on Cassi's other side, her body so stiff she could easily pass as a statue.

Closing her eyes, Cassi ignored Raven. Her body swayed to a melody that only she could hear. Her lips moved, repeating the same words over and over until her voice strengthened and we could all hear her. "Uncloak the soul that needs to be free to rest from the magic that doesn't belong to them."

"We should go." Raven's eyes widened, and she gestured in the direction from which we'd come. "This really could be a trap."

"We're not going anywhere." Kendric clenched his hands into fists. "I'm not moving if we can finally get answers."

Cassi continued to repeat the words, and her voice became even louder, more forceful. The air around us shimmered with iridescent swirls and a cool sensation that put me on edge. It seemed similar to the pressure I experienced when the shadows came at me.

The iridescent sheen flashed like the magic was being impacted.

My jaw ticced.

"It's working!" a male voice called from behind us. "I can see the outline of a body."

Cassi didn't pause. She repeated the words louder and faster. The air shimmered again, her spell weaving tighter around us.

Voice strangled, Raven hissed, "We need to leave. This is dangerous."

I didn't have to ask because I knew none of the wolf shifters would be going anywhere. We needed to see the final reveal, and we could only hope it wasn't a trap.

Cassi's voice rose, and the iridescent waves pulsed outward as if exploding from within. The air fractured before it seemed to crack wide open.

Before us, our enemy lay in plain sight, revealing who it truly was.

The world stopped spinning, the silence so profound we were all holding our breath, trying to comprehend what we were staring at.

All this time, we'd thought it was the Blackwoods.

We'd been so very wrong.

Lying before us was a vampire.

A vampire that smelled like a shifter, albeit faintly.

And the icing on the whole damn cake was...it was the vampire that Ryker and I had believed had saved us the other night from the Blackwoods' attack.

David.

Eyes widening, Briar stumbled back a step. "I don't understand," she whispered.

Unfortunately, I did.

The first vampire for whom I'd let my defenses down was the very one who'd betrayed us.

All at once, every eye turned on Raven, who stood there frozen and paler than a ghost, her dark eyes wide with fear.

"I...I can explain," she rasped.

# ABOUT THE AUTHOR

Jen L. Grey is a *USA Today* Bestselling Author who writes Paranormal Romance, Urban Fantasy, and Fantasy genres.

Jen lives in Tennessee with her husband, two daughters, and three miniature Australian Shepherds. Before she began writing, she was an avid reader and enjoyed being involved in the indie community. Her love for books eventually led her to writing. For more information, please visit her website and sign up for her newsletter.

Check out her future projects and book signing events at
her website.
www.jenlgrey.com

# ALSO BY JEN L. GREY

**Of Fae and Wolf Trilogy**

Bonded to the Fallen Shadow King

**Rejected Fate Trilogy**

Betrayed Mate

Cursed Magic

Wicked Fate

**Fated To Darkness**

The King of Frost and Shadows

The Court of Thorns and Wings

The Kingdom of Flames and Ash

**The Forbidden Mate Trilogy**

Wolf Mate

Wolf Bitten

Wolf Touched

**Standalone Romantasy**

Of Shadows and Fae

**Twisted Fate Trilogy**

Destined Mate

Eclipsed Heart

Chosen Destiny

**The Marked Dragon Prince Trilogy**

Ruthless Mate

Marked Dragon

Hidden Fate

**Shadow City: Silver Wolf Trilogy**

Broken Mate

Rising Darkness

Silver Moon

**Shadow City: Royal Vampire Trilogy**

Cursed Mate

Shadow Bitten

Demon Blood

**Shadow City: Demon Wolf Trilogy**

Ruined Mate

Shattered Curse

Fated Souls

**Shadow City: Dark Angel Trilogy**

Fallen Mate

Demon Marked

Dark Prince

Fatal Secrets

## Shadow City: Silver Mate

Shattered Wolf

Fated Hearts

Ruthless Moon

## The Wolf Born Trilogy

Hidden Mate

Blood Secrets

Awakened Magic

## The Hidden King Trilogy

Dragon Mate

Dragon Heir

Dragon Queen

## The Marked Wolf Trilogy

Moon Kissed

Chosen Wolf

Broken Curse

## Wolf Moon Academy Trilogy

Shadow Mate

Blood Legacy

Rising Fate

## The Royal Heir Trilogy

Wolves' Queen

Wolf Unleashed

Wolf's Claim

## Bloodshed Academy Trilogy

Year One

Year Two

Year Three

## The Half-Breed Prison Duology (Same World As Bloodshed Academy)

Hunted

Cursed

## The Artifact Reaper Series

Reaper: The Beginning

Reaper of Earth

Reaper of Wings

Reaper of Flames

Reaper of Water

## Stones of Amaria (Shared World)

Kingdom of Storms

Kingdom of Shadows

Kingdom of Ruins

Kingdom of Fire

## The Pearson Prophecy

Dawning Ascent

Enlightened Ascent

Reigning Ascent

**Stand Alones**

Death's Angel

Rising Alpha

Made in the USA
Columbia, SC
08 June 2025

59085519R00167